Millie Bontrager

By Strange Paths

ZONDERVAN HEARTH BOOKS

Available from your Christian Bookseller

Book Number		
	Ken Anderson	
1	The Doctor's Return	*A Hearth Romance*
	Francena Arnold	
2	The Deepening Stream	*A Hearth Romance*
3	Fruit for Tomorrow	*A Hearth Romance*
4	Light in My Window	*A Hearth Romance*
	Sallie Lee Bell	
5	The Barrier	*A Hearth Romance*
6	By Strange Paths	*A Hearth Romance*
7	The Last Surrender	*A Hearth Romance*
8	The Long Search	*A Hearth Mystery*
9	Romance Along the Bayou	*A Hearth Romance*
10	The Scar	*A Hearth Romance*
11	The Substitute	*A Hearth Romance*
12	Through Golden Meadows	*A Hearth Romance*
13	Until the Daybreak	*A Hearth Romance*
	Beth Brown	
14	Candle of the Wicked	*A Hearth Mystery*
	Matsu Crawford	
15	Love Is Like an Acorn	*A Hearth Romance*
	Ruth Livingston Hill	
16	This Side of Tomorrow	*A Hearth Romance*
	Guy Howard	
17	Give Me Thy Vineyard	*A Hearth Romance*
	James H. Hunter	
18	The Mystery of Mar Saba	*A Hearth Mystery*
	N.I. Saloff-Astakhoff	
19	Judith	*A Hearth Romance*
	Lon Woodrum	
20	Trumpets in the Morning	*A Hearth Romance*

A HEARTH ROMANCE

By Strange Paths

Sallie Lee Bell

OF THE ZONDERVAN CORPORATION | GRAND RAPIDS, MICHIGAN 49506

First Zondervan Books edition 1974
Fifth printing 1975
Sixth printing 1976

Printed in the U.S.A.

CHAPTER 1

Dusk was falling like a thin gray mantle over Paris, making the narrow streets in the slum section of the city dark avenues of danger for one who was not a dweller there.

Elise Demarest shut the door of the shabby tenement and stepped out into the gathering darkness. She was not thinking of possible danger that might lurk in dark doorways or meet her around a corner. Her thoughts were upon the woman she had left in the small dirty room, a woman who would soon be slipping out into eternity and, but for the grace of God, into a Christless eternity.

How glad Elise was that she had come, even though she had been so tired and the way had seemed so long. She could still hear the echo of the woman's weak voice as she greeted her.

"I was so afraid you wouldn't come," she had gasped from lungs rapidly failing.

"I couldn't stay away when I knew you wanted me to come," Elise had answered, kneeling by the pallet and taking the thin, bloodless hand in hers.

"Now tell me more," the woman urged. "I'm slipping away fast and time is short. I'm afraid to die. Tell me more."

Elise reached into her pocket and pulled out a worn, vellum-bound Bible. It was the one treasure she had inherited from her mother; a precious possession, but a dangerous one to own at a time like this when true believers were still in danger of being persecuted for their belief in God and His Word.

She had read to the dying woman passages that had become precious to her and had pointed out the way of salvation as simply as she could. Once before she had tried to talk to this same woman when both of them were working together in one of the shops, Elise as a salesgirl and the other as a scrub woman. But the woman had only laughed at her and jeered at her message and had hinted that prisons and scaffolds were made for such heretics as she. Elise had given out the Word, however, and God's promise had proved true: His Word did not return unto Him void. The Word had taken root in the woman's heart and now, in the hour of death, with the fear of the unknown eternity facing her, she had sent for Elise. Remembering her scoffing, she had feared that the girl would not come.

Elise recalled, with a sigh of happiness, the slow smile that had spread over the wan face of the woman as she had finally seen the truth and as the light of eternal life shone into her heart. She knew that very likely she would never see the woman again on earth, but there was no doubt in her heart that one day they would meet again at the feet of the Saviour who was now theirs together.

She was so engrossed in her thoughts that she did not realize how dark it had grown. The dim street lamps only added to the gloom of the dark narrow streets beyond the faint glow of light. She realized that no part of Paris was safe for a girl alone at night and that this was one of the worst districts of the city, but she was not afraid. She felt that she was in the service of her King and that His presence would protect her from possible harm.

As if to mock her trust in that unseen Presence, as she turned a corner two men slipped out from an obscure doorway and seized her. Before she could cry out, a dirty hand struck her mouth shut and bruised her lips. A harsh voice warned her, "If you know what's good for you, you'll come with us quietly. We'd hate to have to get rough with you, but we will if you don't come quietly."

She couldn't have done otherwise, with that hand covering her mouth almost choking her. There was no use to struggle; a pair of strong arms held her own arms close to her side. The men hustled her into a house nearby, down a dark hallway and into a room. Releasing her, they left, after they had shut the door and locked it. She heard the tramp of heavy feet and then the closing of an outer door.

Everything had happened so quickly that for a moment the girl was stunned, but as she regained her composure somewhat, she looked about her in the dim light shed by a smoking candle. There were seven or eight other girls there and they were looking at her with dull stares. She stared back at them, silently, wonderingly. They were an evil looking lot. They were young, some of them seemingly younger than herself, but on their faces was stamped the unmistakable marks of dissipation and sin. Some of them were dressed in garish evening dresses with buffant skirts and tight bodices. They must have been on their way to some dance hall. Others were dressed in street clothes. Some of these looked fairly decent; others were dirty and unkempt and bleary-eyed, as if they had just emerged from intoxication and had gone out for another glass of liquor or a breath of fresh air.

Finally one of them spoke. "Well," she drawled,

"finished sizing us up? What do you think of us? Pretty sorry looking bunch of bums, aren't we?"

"I — I — wasn't sizing you up," Elise stammered. "I was just wondering what this all means. What are we all doing here? How did you get here?"

"The same way you did, I suppose," the other answered. "Some dirty night prowler stepped out of a doorway and clapped his hand over my mouth while the other fellow grabbed me and dragged me here. I tried to kick the shins off him, but every time I kicked he slapped me. So — well, here I am."

"What are they going to do with us?" Elise asked.

"How do we know? They didn't tell us that. Why didn't you ask him? He might have told you. You look like a lady." The girl laughed mirthlessly as she turned her bloodshot eyes upon Elise's lovely face.

At this point the door opened and another girl was unceremoniously shoved into the room. She was young and rather pretty. She cried softly as they left her lying where she had fallen. As the door closed behind her and the heavy feet tramped down the hall, the girl turned over and hid her face in the curve of her arm and gave way to unrestrained grief.

Impulsively Elise knelt beside her and put her hand upon the girl's head.

"Don't cry, dear, that won't help," she whispered. "I'm sure we'll all get out of this somehow. God will help us, I'm sure."

"God!" echoed the girl who had spoken to Elise before. The very tone of her voice was so full of scorn and venom that Elise shuddered. "What's He got to do with this? This is the devil's world. I ought to know. God's turned the world over to him. Don't you know that? We all belong to the devil anyway. But who cares?"

"I care," Elise answered quietly, "and I know God cares."

"H'm. Funny talk. Say, who are you? What's your name?"

"Elise Demarest. What's yours?" Elise smiled as she asked the question, but there was no answering smile upon the lips of the other.

"Just call me Annette," she said in harsh tones. "I don't want to remember the rest of my name. When a girl's mother sends her out to sell herself for a few drinks, she wants to forget that mother."

The girl on the floor had been forgotten for the moment. She ceased crying and sat up, listening to the conversation while the tears still hung upon her wet lashes.

"That's why I'm here tonight," she finally blurted out. "My father sent me out to bring in money so that he could get the liquor he's too lazy to work for. My mother just died last night and he wanted to get drunk so that he could forget that he had helped to kill her. When I was on my way to the cafe those two grabbed me. But what does it matter what happens to me? My mother is dead and I hate my father!" Her sobs broke out afresh.

The door opened again and the two men came in and surveyed the group.

"I'm warning you girls that if one of you tries to break away, she'll get a knife in her back," one of the men said. His evil eyes scanned their faces. Then he spoke again, "Line up over there. Now turn your backs."

The girls obeyed. Their hands were then tied behind their backs and their eyes blindfolded.

"Where are you taking us?" asked Annette. "There's a law against what you're doing."

"Shut up, or you'll wish you had." The man gave her a slap across her mouth that brought the blood from her swollen lips. "Who cares for law? We've got orders and we get paid for what we do, so you'd best go with us and not give us any trouble or it'll be the last time you do."

The girls were gagged and tied to each other with ropes about their waists. After they had been led outside, they were ordered to climb into a cart. The cart was small and they were forced to stand, crowded in like a bunch of cattle on the way to the slaughter pen. Over the rough cobble stones they jolted. The cart turned one corner after another until finally it stopped. Ordered to get out of the cart, they slipped and fell over one another while the men cursed them and jerked them roughly to their feet.

Elise could hear the lapping of water, and she knew from the steep ladder they were forced to climb that they were going aboard a ship. Still blindfolded, they were taken below deck and huddled into the dark hold of the ship. After a while someone came and cut the ropes around their waists and hands, took off the blindfolds and removed the gags.

Annette was the first to speak. "We're on board a ship," she whispered. Her lips and throat were parched after the long continued gagging.

"Yes, I heard the water before we left the cart," Elise replied.

"We're being shipped away!" cried another of the girls.

"Where to, do you suppose?" cried another.

"Being taken off to slavery, no doubt. Such things have happened."

"No!" cried Elise. "I don't believe it."

"Why not?" demanded Annette. "Didn't those beasts say they were being paid for capturing us? What else would they want to ship us off for?"

"I don't believe God would let that happen to us," Elise said.

"God!" Again Annette spoke in ridicule. "What's He got to do with this? What's He ever done for me but make my life misery itself? Why wouldn't He let us be sold into slavery? It would be no worse than what we've lived in back there in Paris."

"Because I trust Him and I know He'll keep me safe." Elise faced the other's scornful voice in the darkness and though Annette could not see, there glowed a light in the lovely girl's eyes that was not of earth, not of the slime and filth and sin which the other's eyes had beheld for so long.

"You do? mocked Annette's voice. "Well, while He's keeping you so safe, what about the rest of us?"

Elise hesitated a moment, then spoke with quiet assurance. "Once when the Apostle Paul was on a ship and a prisoner, just as we are, there was a terrible storm and everyone except him thought that the ship would sink; but he trusted God and God gave him not only his own life but also those with him in the ship."

"And so, because you believe in God, you believe He'll deliver us all?"

The derision and unholy mirth in her voice provoked Elise to reply, "I know He is able and I shall trust Him to deliver us. God loves each one of you whether you believe in Him or not."

"I don't want His love!" Annette's voice rose to a shriek. "What kind of a love would let me suffer until I've lost all feeling but hate? Don't tell me about God!" A string of oaths fell from her lips.

Elise shuddered, but from her heart went up a silent prayer that God would forgive Annette and, however strange the way, lead her to Him.

Annette's outburst had brought silence. Finally the girls drifted one by one into the sleep of exhaustion.

CHAPTER 2

The girls awakened to the tossing of the ship in a choppy sea. A dim light filtered to them through an open hatch and they observed that they were not alone in the hold. Other girls had been there when they had arrived. All of them were pitifully drab and bedraggled. Their cheap dresses with ruffles and lace were rumpled and soiled. Their hair hung in disorder about faces that were sallow and haggard not only from a dissolute life, but from the seasickness which assailed many of them in ever increasing waves of nausea.

Presently someone came down through the open hatch and led them to the deck above where the fresh air revived some of them and the nausea at length passed. Others less hardy clung to the nearest object or lay stretched upon the deck, moaning and cursing at the strange fate that had brought them to this desperate plight.

Elise stood by the rail looking at the shoreline, now just a faint blue streak in the distance. They had come out of the channel into the open sea where the waves were rolling effortlessly and over long expanses. The sails spread themselves full to the brisk breeze which bore the ship along ahead of a white trail of foam.

The wind curled Elise's golden-brown hair in soft tendrils about her face. Brown eyes under long lashes gazed wistfully out over the widening expanse which separated their owner from her homeland.

The girl cupped her dimpled chin in her small hands and rested her elbows upon the rough wooden railing. Why had this happened to her and where were they taking her? Who had done this terrible thing? She had been upon a mission of mercy, carrying the love of God to an unlovely soul. She had believed God's promise that "the angel of the Lord encampeth round about them that fear Him and delivereth them." Where had the angel been when those vile men had taken her captive?

Her hand touched the pocket concealed in her full skirt. She felt the little book which she had put there when she had left the sick woman's room. Of all her few possessions, this Book was the one thing she treasured most. It had been a source of comfort to her in an hour of bereavement when her mother had died so suddenly and she was left alone to face a world which regarded her kind as heretics, fit only for torture and death.

She turned and looked at the other girls who were some distance away. Those who were not still sick were sitting apathetically on the deck, too weary and worn to care where they were or how they looked. A great wave of compassion swept over her for these sin-stricken girls who looked so utterly hopeless and miserable. They didn't have the source of comfort which she possessed. They had no hope of a future which grew brighter as one approached it. Living only for the sordid present, without hope and without a solid foundation upon which to base any hope, they had only the torment of a soul which could find no peace and of a conscience which must sometimes bring pain even though it might be dulled. She longed to try in some way to bring a word to them from the Word of Life but after her experience with Annette she dared not make the attempt.

Her gaze wandered to Annette, who was among the ones who had just recovered from the worst of the attack of seasickness. Her face was a sickly green; her eyes, dull and glassy, stared vacantly before her as she lay against a pile of rope. The rising sun brought into pitiful light every line of her haggard face. The younger girl, Claire, who had wept so bitterly the night before, was not far from Annette. She was too ill to open her eyes, and lay white and still, the stillness interrupted at intervals by violent retching.

Elise strolled over to one side of the ship where there was a spot of shade and sat down upon a box. Except for the sailors manning the vessel, she had not seen any man but the silent individual who had taken them out of the hold on to the deck. She took out her Bible and idly turned the pages. She was looking for some verse which would give her the comfort so sorely needed in this hour of uncertainty and vague fear of the unknown. She couldn't believe that her Lord would let her be sold into slavery; yet in the light of what had happened and remembering Annette's words, she couldn't find any other conclusion.

As she turned the pages her eye fell upon a verse in Proverbs. She read it slowly for she hadn't remembered reading it before: "In the way of righteousness is life and in the pathway thereof there is no death." She read it over and over again; it was new to her. She could find no better promise than this, no matter how long she searched. She was going somewhere, she knew not where. The way was new and strange, but she knew from the promise that there could be but one end to that pathway — there would be no death but eternal life. A new sense of peace filled her soul, a peace which took away all doubt and fear of the unknown. If she was in the way of righteousness, in God's will, even though suffering and physical death might come, there would be glorious life throughout all eternity waiting for her at the end. It was what her mother had tried to teach her in those hours of danger, when they knew not what moment they might become the victims of some lawless mob, their life ended through torture or the stake. She had tried to accept and understand, but not until this moment had she really been put to the test.

She raised her eyes from the page and sighed. Tranquillity illumined her face, suffusing it with a radiance that made it beautiful. A sailor passed at that moment and saw her thus, her lips moving in words of silent prayer. He gave her a casual glance; then turned and looked again, stopped and stared at her in surprise. She reminded him of pictures of saints he had seen in the dim cathedrals when he was a child. But those saints couldn't compare with the beauty of this girl with the petal-like complexion and the piquant face so untouched by the sordid worldliness which marked the faces of the others on deck.

He strolled back to where she sat and watched her for a moment as she sat there unconscious of his presence. His voice startled her.

"Recitin' your prayers?" he asked.

Her startled eyes met his and what she saw there brought color to her cheeks.

"No, I wasn't reciting any prayer. I was just thanking God for His goodness to me," she answered, trying to avoid his stare.

"H'm. What can your kind find to thank God for?" he questioned as he pointed a thumb at the girls grouped on the after deck.

"I can thank Him for saving me from being one of them," she replied.

The leer disappeared from his face as though it had

no right to be there. "You're different from them all right," he admitted. "How did you get mixed up with that riffraff?"

"I was on my way home from visiting a sick woman when two men seized me and threw me into the room where they were. I never saw any of them before."

"It's a rotten business," he stated. "I heard they were shanghaiing girls but I didn't believe they'd get anyone like you. They made a mistake, I guess, but it's too late now." There was a note of sympathy in his voice.

"Where are they taking us?" she asked as a faint fear again assailed her.

"To new Orleans. Ever hear of it?"

She nodded. "What are they going to do with us?"

"Marry you off to the fellows who need wives and can't find 'em. Women are scarce in the colony and the Company agreed to get wives for them if they'd stay on and help build the colony."

She stared at him open-mouthed. "They can't do that!" she cried.

"No? Just wait and see. I'll bet those others'll think it's the best break they've had yet. It ain't often that their kind manage to get a husband hooked. Now they'll have their pick. And some of those fellows in New Orleans have plenty of money."

Just then there was a call from forward and the sailor hurried off to his post, leaving Elise the victim of conflicting emotions. She found a measure of relief in the sailor's words. At least they were not to be sold as slaves. She sat with her open Bible upon her lap but her eyes were not upon the printed page. What would become of her in this strange new land, without friends, without money, without even a change of clothes? What would they do to her when they found that they had made a mistake and that she was not willing to be married off to some person she had never seen before? That would be little better than slavery. But she had the promise in that verse and she clung to it.

Presently another member of the crew came toward her and she slipped the book back into her pocket. She didn't want that taken from her.

"You girls come on down below and I'll show you where you're to stay during the voyage," he called as he came nearer.

Most of the girls were able to walk, though Claire staggered weakly and would have fallen if Elise had not steadied her with an arm about her waist. They were led below to where there were a number of crude bunks. These were assigned to the girls and they were told that breakfast would be ready shortly. Now that they were out at sea there was no danger of discovery and they could be given their freedom. Elise was thankful that she would not have to spend another night in that foul hold.

There was a basin of water on a stand in the passageway near the bunk rooms and a bucket of water beside it. The girls took turns washing their faces and making themselves as presentable as possible. One of them had a comb in her pocket and they all used it to rearrange their hair.

"I saw you talking to that sailor," Annette remarked as she stood by Elise in line waiting for her turn at the basin. "Did you find out what they're going to do with us?" It was the first time she had said anything to her since her outburst before they boarded the ship.

"Yes. He said we're bound for New Orleans."

"Where's that?" asked one of the others.

"It's in the colony of Louisiana in America," Elise informed her.

"What are they going to do with us when they get us there?" Annette asked impatiently.

"We're to be married to the settlers."

"Married!" Annette burst into harsh laughter. "That is a joke! Instead of slaves, we're to be brides. Do we pick our husbands or do they pick us?"

"I don't know. He didn't tell me that."

"What do you think of the idea?" Annette wanted to know.

"I think it's terrible! We're not animals!" Elise's voice was tense.

"H'm. I don't think it's so terrible. It may be a pretty good end to a bad beginning." Annette shrugged her shoulders. "We've got nothing to lose and we might get a pleasant surprise."

Elise didn't reply but took her turn at the basin and with the much-used comb. She didn't like the idea of using the comb but there was nothing else to do.

Annette noticed her hesitation. "If the comb ain't good enough, just don't use it," she remarked. Elise let the gibe pass.

As the breakfast summons came, the women filed into the forward part of the ship where meals were served. As they took their places on the benches alongside the table, Elise hesitated a moment, then bowed her head and returned silent thanks before the meal was served. She could feel eyes upon her and she knew they were thinking things that perhaps they would say later on. Her face was flushed when she raised her head and faced their curious stares, but she pretended not to notice as the food was passed and they began to eat.

"What were you doing?" whispered Claire who sat beside her.

"Just thanking God for the food I was about to eat," Elise told her.

"Why should you thank God for this stuff?" There was the same bitter note in her voice that Elise had heard in Annette's.

"It's better than nothing, isn't it?" and Elise gave her a bright smile.

"H'm — maybe. But I don't see what God's got to do with it. What did He ever do for you?"

"He died on the Cross for me." Elise was hoping that her remarks to Claire would be the right ones.

"I've heard that before," remarked Claire skeptically. This time there was no sneer in the girl's voice.

"He made it possible for me to receive eternal life. He made it possible for you too, Claire," she added softly.

"Who wants eternal life?" Claire shot back in low bitter tones. "I don't want to live. I wish I could die."

"That's easy to do," Elise told her. "Just jump overboard and you'll be dead in no time at all."

"But I — I — don't want to drown," Claire protested. "I'd be afraid," she admitted.

Elise smiled. "Sure you would. You're afraid because you don't know what lies on the other side of death. The Lord died on the Cross so that you wouldn't have to be afraid of death."

"You're not afraid to die, of course." There was ridicule in the girl's voice.

Elise shook her head.

"Pooh! I don't believe you," Claire scoffed and turned her attention to her breakfast.

Just two days later Claire had occasion to remember Elise's words. The sea had been unusually calm. The wind barely billowed the sails. Most of the time they hung slack and empty and the booms groaned and creaked with the slow swell of the sea. The sky that morning had been red and lowering and the captain had stood on the bridge beside the pilot most of the day, scanning the distant horizon for signs of approaching bad weather.

It came toward sundown, first with a breeze that swept the sails far out over the side of the ship. As the sailors sprang to their posts, reefing the sails as rapidly as possible, the girls stood grouped on the after deck watching them, all unconscious of approaching danger. Time bore heavily on their hands. One of them had found a deck of cards and they played at intervals, passing the deck from one group to another, but they had tired of that and were wondering moodily how long the monotonous voyage would last. They had been told that it depended upon the weather.

The storm came with black clouds scudding across a darkening sky, while the waves whipped higher and higher until they became mountainous billows which seemed poised, ready to rush upon them like mighty monsters seeking to devour them.

The girls were ordered below deck at the first onslaught of the wind. They sat in huddled groups wondering how long the ship could hold out against the furious battle of the elements. Some of them became sick again, but the others became more and more frightened as the ship rolled and tossed like an egg shell in the trough of the waves, or rose on the crest only to be plunged down to the depths once more.

Elise sat apart from the others. They had left her to herself, for she wouldn't join their card games nor take any part in their bawdy songs and lewd jokes. Once or twice she had attempted to join in their conversation when they discussed decent subjects, but they gave her to understand that they wanted nothing to do with her, so she kept to herself, feeling more lonely as the days passed and the uncertain future loomed nearer. Even Claire had shunned her.

As the fury of the storm increased the girls began to cry out in terror. Some of them crossed themselves and muttered words they had learned long ago before sin had set its seal upon them. Since none of them had ever been to sea before, the storm seemed more terrible than it was in reality. At each violent lurch of the ship they thought that they would be hurled to the depths below; and as the ship rocked in its battle with the elements, they felt as if it would be torn apart. Elise wondered if this was to be the end of the voyage for them all. She sat there in the dimly lighted room calm and silent while the others moaned or cried aloud in their fright. Her whole physical being shrank from the prospect of death by drowning, yet she knew that if that were to be the end of the path, there could be nothing but good remaining. Her Lord would be there to carry her through the dark valley of the waters if they should claim her life and after the dark valley there would be the light of eternity and joy forevermore.

She had been so lonely since her mother's death and life had held little promise of happiness for her. It had stretched out as a long road over which she must travel alone, and the struggle for existence sometimes seemed greater than she could bear. As she sat there, tossed about by the pitching of the ship, reviewing her past life and looking toward the future beyond the surging waves, a new sense of exhilaration took possession of her, a sense of joy and peace which she had never felt before. She had told Claire that she would not be afraid to die, but she had said that only in theory. Now she was facing death and she was not afraid. If death did not come, she could know through all the years that life might hold that through Him who had conquered death, the fear of it was forever taken from her.

She turned and looked at the others. They were sitting in grotesque groups, trying to steady themselves against the violent tossing of the boat. Near her lay Claire, stretched upon the floor, too sick to sit up, but moaning weakly and crying out at each plunge of the ship into the trough of the waves. She went over to the moaning girl and knelt beside her, steadying herself with her hands upon the floor.

"Isn't there something I can do for you, Claire?" she asked. "Will you let me bathe your face? It might help a little."

"No. No!" Claire sobbed. "Let me alone. Let me die! We'll all be drowned anyway. But I'm afraid to die. Afraid!"

"If you'd let me, I could tell you how you wouldn't need to be afraid. Will you let me tell you?" Elsie begged.

"No! Go away! Let me alone!" and the girl turned her face away as a violent fit of nausea gripped her.

Toward morning the wind began to die down and the ship rocked less violently. Elise suggested that they should go to bed, but none of them paid any attention to her. They lay huddled in exhausted heaps upon the floor or else propped against the walls of the room. She went to her bunk and was soon fast asleep.

At breakfast-time those who were able to come to the table were a much chastened, bedraggled group. Claire came in and took her seat beside Elise. She was wan and holloweyed and could eat but little.

As the others left the table she lingered behind for a word with Elise.

"I'm sorry I was cross with you last night," she said. "Please forgive me."

"Of course," Elise assured her. "I shouldn't have bothered you, but I was so anxious to share the peace in my heart with you."

"Some day, if we ever get to New Orleans, I want you to tell me about it," the girl said. "I want to know what it was that kept you from being afraid. I didn't believe you when you said you weren't afraid to die, but now I know you were telling me the truth."

“Why not let me tell you now,” Elise offered.

“No. Not now. They would laugh at me like they laugh at you, and I couldn’t stand that.” Then she left Elise to join the others.

CHAPTER 3

The days passed in monotonous succession after the interlude of the storm while the *Sea Rover* made its slow passage to New Orleans. The girls walked the decks or sat in disgruntled groups, too bored and dispirited to talk. They had tired of one another's company. They had even tired of their endless card games and there was nothing else to do but walk or sit and look out over the sea. They were kept on the afterdeck and were not allowed to have any communication with the crew. They managed to keep themselves clean by taking turns washing each other's undergarments; but their dresses were much soiled and rumpled, for the flimsy silk or satin which they had been wearing wouldn't stand washing. Elise still had a daintiness and freshness about her which the others noted but which seemed to make them dislike her more. The dress she had worn was of cotton and she had washed its not too full skirt and bodice, keeping herself clean while they grew more bedraggled in their worn finery.

At last the ship wound its way up the river and approached New Orleans. As it came within sight of the settlement, the girls lost their lethargy and stood close to the rail, chattering in excited groups. They had made themselves as presentable as possible and were waiting impatiently for the boat to tie up at the landing. Elise stood apart from the rest, her sombre eyes looking over the muddy waters toward the settlement which dignified itself by the name of *Nouvelle Orleans.*

Willows were waving green plumes along the batture outside the low embankment which protected the city from the semi-annual rise of the river. As they eased into the rudely constructed quay which projected out over the batture and was protected by palisades from the eddying stream, she could see that the levee and the open square of the Place d' Armes was crowded by a strange conglomeration of humanity. Practically the whole male population of the settlement was on the levee or just beyond it, to watch the ship with its unusual cargo.

There had been shiploads of immigrants landing there before, many of them not willing emigrants but victims who had been ruthlessly snatched away from their homes as the girls had been, by the scheming tricksters who had started the stampede to the new colony under the orders of John Law and his unscrupulous leaders in the Mississippi Company. Now these same colonists who had been lured or been forced to become citizens of this settlement were becoming so restless and embittered by the dying of their hopes and dreams that the Company had had to promise wives for them in order to keep them from leaving the colony bereft of the men needed to keep it going. Now that the promised wives had arrived, there was as much excitement on land as there was on board the ship.

Elise noted that many of the citizens were dressed in the prevailing Paris fashion — knee breeches, silk stockings, pumps with silver buckles. Some of them even wore wigs carefully curled. Others were dressed in homespun with trousers that were much worn.

Their bare heads revealed hair that was neither curled nor powdered. Here and there in the crowd was a dark-skinned Indian with leather leggings and much-painted body. Elise was fascinated by these Indians and tried to imagine what thoughts were passing behind their stern faces.

Over to one side, a little apart from the others who stood nearest the wharf, were two men. One of them was dressed in silk with knee breeches and high-heeled slippers, bright waistcoat and ruffled shirt front. He was thin and of medium height. His black hair ran smoothly back from the rather high forehead. His narrow face and high cheek bones, the straight brow and thin lips marked the calm ruthlessness of the man; and though he was fairly handsome, the cold eyes robbed his face of whatever charm it might possess.

When they drew alongside, Elise realized suddenly that he was looking at her. Those steel gray eyes were appraising her and the look she saw in them brought sudden color to her face. She was made aware once more that she was a part of the bedraggled brides who were waiting for someone to claim them. A surge of anger swept over her and she stared for a moment into those gray eyes, and a defiant light flashed in her own eyes. It brought the shadow of a smile to the man's face.

"Spunky little thing," he remarked to the man beside him.

She turned her gaze to the other man. He was dressed in the garb of a *coureur de bois* — white buckskin leggings, cotton shirt open at the throat and a coon skin cap hanging on the back of his head. His hair was reddish brown and his sun-tanned face was ruggedly handsome, with hazel eyes, a generous mouth and a chin with a deep cleft in it that gave him a little-boy look which was intensified when his lips parted in a smile. He too was looking at her but the look was so frankly admiring that she dropped her eyes and turned away.

"She's a beauty," the *coureur de bois* replied. "I wouldn't mind having a wife if I could get her."

The other smiled. "Why don't you try to get her? But if you did, you'd have to stay at home more than you do now and keep an eye on her, or someone else might run off with her. She's to pretty to be left alone while you go roaming the woods."

"I'd have to keep an eye on you, if I got out of sight of home," his companion retorted. "I saw the way you were sizing her up. Don't get any ideas about her, because I think I'm going to get her. I'll try anyway. What I want I usually get."

The other didn't answer, for the boat had tied up and the gang plank was being lowered. The girls were marched down the gang plank and across the levee toward the Rue Royal. Men leered at them or stared with curious eyes as the long line of girls passed, guarded by gendarmes from the fort. Elise longed to be able to hide her face from these boldly staring eyes and the eager appraising gaze of those who stood nearby while she passed. Claire was beside her and the girl clutched her arm and murmured, "Elise, I'm afraid. Some of those men look terrible. I don't want to marry any one of them."

"You don't have to," Elise assured her. "You're not a slave and they can't make you marry without your consent."

"If we don't marry, what'll become of us? We don't have any money or even any clothes."

"I don't know," Elise was forced to admit. She had been asking herself the same question.

As they left the *Place d' armes* and crossed the dusty street with its board banquette, the crowd followed them. Past the Market Place on the side of the Square and up a couple of streets, then the gendarmes stopped before a big house of white plaster between cypress uprights. There were large windows covered by thin cloth and a stout door at the head of the wide front stairs. The door was opened by a nun in answer to the knock of one of the gendarmes and the girls were led inside; then the door was closed and locked behind them.

They stood in the large double parlors of the house while the black-robed nun conferred with the soldiers.

Annette remarked, “Well, this is the end of the journey. Now for the wedding.” Her lips were parted in a bitter smile.

CHAPTER 4

In the bright sunlight of an August morning, Monsieur Andre Damont walked leisurely down the Rue Chartres toward Rue St. Anne. At the corner he turned to his left and continued until he came within sight of the large house that had housed the girls. A cart rumbled down the street drawn by a sickly looking mule which kicked up a cloud of dust as it trudged lazily along toward the Market Place. Monsieur Damont cast an annoyed glance at the driver of the cart as he flecked the dust from his satin sleeve and continued on his way.

He was dressed, as usual, in an immaculate white ruffled shirt under a satin waistcoat and long-tailed coat of dark blue. His short trousers were adorned with silver buckles resting upon a knot of blue ribbon and his thin legs were encased in black silk stockings. Upon his face there was a self-satisfied expression and his thin lips were parted in a faint smile. He was thinking that he had managed this little affair rather well on such short notice. Until the coming of the ship with its unusual cargo another affair of his was giving him no little worry. Rosalie Allain was getting more pronounced in her attitude toward him and he didn't want to run the risk of a duel with her stupid husband, for though Allain was stupid he was one of the best swordsmen in the colony. But Rosalie possessed a strong fascination for him which he knew would inevitably be the means of his downfall if he could not manage to escape the net which she was slowly but surely weaving about him. He didn't love her but she was beautiful and she loved him. With no other woman in the colony who could either hold his interest or offer some diversion from a monotonous life, he was becoming more and more involved in this dangerous situation. The first glimpse of Elise told him that he had found the solution to this problem. If he were safely married, Rosalie would not dare pursue him too openly and he felt that he would soon be free from her dangerous lure.

There was still the problem of the Indian girl, White Dove, whom he had married last year, but she presented no real barrier to his plans. He had married her acording to the rites of her own tribe and if he wished, he could just forget her. It had been done by others before. She was beautiful in her dark sombre way and she had proved a diverting interlude when life became too dull in town. She was content to stay with her own people, with a visit now and then from him. No one else knew about his Indian wife and he told himself that no one need ever know. She would be just a past incident.

Although he thought that Elise was like the others, part of the riff-raff and underworld of Paris, she was beautiful and the withering look she had given him from the deck of the ship told him that she had spirit. Life with her might not be too dull. If it was, there were ways of getting rid of her. She had stirred his emotions even in that brief glimpse of her in a way that he had not thought possible.

He possessed influence with the officers of the Mississippi Company which had had the girls brought over, so it did not take too much maneuvering to get the desired ticket which gave him access to the girls who would be taken as wives. It took a little more maneuvering and some money, of which he had quite enough, to have her left until the last. He didn't want to run the risk of having some other fellow get there ahead of him and go away with the prize bride of them all.

He smiled broadly as he thought of Andre Chenier, the *coureur de bois* who had been so boastful at the landing. Andre had said that he wanted this girl and had boasted that what he wanted he usually got. Well, this would be one time that friend Andre would fail. Andre Chenier was safely tucked away for the time being in the small jail of the town. By the time he was freed, the girl would be married and she would be out of reach.

Monsieur Damont's thoughts were interrupted by the sound of a heavy step behind him. He turned to see Monsieur Andre Chenier in person. He tried to conceal his surprise and his chagrin as the other approached him.

"Where do you think you're going?" Chenier wanted to know as he caught up with him.

"Is that any of your affair?" Damont asked, clearly implying that it was not.

"I intend to make it my affair," cried Chenier belligerently. "And what's more, I'm going to make it my business to find out who had me locked up in the calaboose on a charge of disorderly drunkenness. I wasn't drunk and those stupid fools who locked me up knew it. They had orders from someone to get me out of the way for some reason. Seeing you here makes me wonder if you didn't have something to do with it."

"Why should I have any concern with what you do?" A faint smile broadened Damont's thin lips. "If you want to get drunk and go on a rampage, don't blame me if you get locked up. That's the new edict of Bienville, not mine."

"You're going in there to get one of those girls, the one I want," Chenier told him. "Otherwise you wouldn't be here at this time of day."

"Are there any girls left?" asked Damont innocently. "I thought they were all married off already."

"You know there's one left. It's the girl we were talking about on the levee. I found out that much. That's why I came here. I'm going to get her or know the reason why. I've got a ticket and I've a right to her. You don't have any ticket, so you may as well not waste your time."

"You're mistaken, my friend," drawled Damont. "I do have a ticket. And it is the last number on the list. I fancy that your number has long since been called."

"You arranged that too, didn't you?" There was an angry spark in the hazel eyes. "Well, I'll show you a thing or two. It takes more than scheming from the likes of you to get ahead of Andre Chenier."

Before Damont was aware of what was happening, Chenier had pushed him aside, almost upsetting him, and stormed through the unlocked door of the big house and out of sight. Damont followed leisurely. He knew that his plans would not be upset by this blustering fellow and he could afford to keep his dignity and bide his time.

Within the house Elise was sitting in one of the back rooms wondering when the final test of her courage would come and how she would face the future after she had met the issue. When the girls had had breakfast the morning after their arrival, they were given clean clothes and a bath. Then they were each given a ticket with a number. The man who had the matching number would meet them in the big parlor of the house and each girl would be given a chance to say yes or no to the prospective husband. There were so many more eager men than there were girls that the Company could afford to let them, in a measure, choose their husbands. It had not taken long for the whole sickening business to be disposed of and only Elise was left to await she knew not what.

She had seen that she had the last number on the list when the numbers were given out and she sent up a little prayer of thangsgiving for that. It would be easier for her, after the others were gone, to take the stand she intended to take. Annette had gone away smiling for the first time since Elise had met her. The prospect of a home, no matter how humble, and someone to provide for her, had offered something which she had never thought possible for her and some of the bitterness had gone out of her as she went away with her future husband to await the marriage ceremony. Claire had been made happy by meeting a young fellow who seemed a little less hardened by sin than the others and who seemed really interested in the girl. She was rather pretty and much younger than the others. She had whispered to Elise before she left that some day she wanted Elise to come to see her and discuss with her about what they had talked about on board the ship.

Elise was startled by the sound of loud voices in the room nearby.

"My name's Andre Chenier," she heard someone say, "and I demand an interview with Mademoiselle. I know she's here and I have a ticket so I'm going to stay until I see her."

"Not so fast, young man," interposed the voice of a nun. "Mademoiselle has a number which does not correspond to yours. I can't let you see her. You should have been here when your number was called."

"How could I be here when someone had me locked in the calaboose?" the furious Chenier responded. "She's here and I have a ticket and I'm going to see her, so send her in here."

Just then the door opened and Damont entered.

"What's all the fuss, sister?" he asked.

"This fellow demands to see Mademoiselle," the nun told him. "I tried to tell him that he was too late but he refuses to go."

"If I'm too late, what's he doing here?" demanded Chenier.

"He has the ticket which corresponds to Mademoiselle's," the nun told him, eyeing him coldly. "You will please leave, Monsieur. There are no more girls."

"There's one left and I'm going to see her," Chenier persisted. "I'll not leave here until I do."

"Be more respectful when you speak to the sister," Damont advised. "You were asked to leave, so you'd best go before there's trouble. You wouldn't want that, would you?" The sneer in Damont's voice was unmistakable.

"I'd love it if it gave me a chance to take care of you!" Chenier told him. "I've been wanting to do that for a long time. You seem to think that because you wear silk and velvet and have a little influence with the governor that you can lord it over me, but I'll fix you so that even if you do have the right number on your ticket, you'll be such a sight that the girl won't even take a second look at you. Do you want to try me out and see if I can really do it?"

"Not here," Damont replied. "Just now I have more important business. Would you mind bringing the girl out, sister, so that I can talk to her."

"What about him?" and the nun indicated Chenier with a jerk of her head.

"He'll leave or he'll land back in the calaboose.

I'll call a guard and have him arrested for disturbing the peace here. Go and get the girl."

"You take one step toward that door and I'll knife you before you reach it," Chenier threatened and drew a long, vicious looking knife from his belt.

Damont's face became a shade paler and the nun uttered a frightened cry.

"Put up that knife," she cried. "Don't you know that would be murder?"

Chenier laughed harshly. "Sure I know it, so if you don't want to see it happen here, bring out the girl and let's see which one she prefers."

As the nun approached the door, Elise waited with fast beating heart for the door to open.

"Come with me," the nun said. "Two gentlemen want to see you."

She followed the nun and stood in the doorway of the parlor. She recognized the two who faced her as the same who had been watching her from the levee. She said nothing but stood there waiting for them to speak. For a moment there was silence in the big room for each man was staring at her in silent admiration. In the simple dark dress with the white collar and with her hair hanging in lose curls about her charming face, she was lovely enough to arrest the attention of any man. To these two who had been so long in this colony where feminine youth and beauty were at such a high premium, she seemed unbelievably lovely.

Andre Chenier was the first to break the silence. "Mademoiselle, I — I — would like to talk to you alone for just a little while, but these two here would never let me. But I saw you on the ship and I — I — well, I wanted to marry you. I've never wanted to marry anyone before, but you're the most beautiful girl I've ever laid eyes on. Give me a chance, won't you? This fellow here dressed in all his finery says he holds the number of your ticket, but he got it by cheating. Give me a chance, won't you?" All of his bluster had left him and in the face of her calm gaze he was suddenly abashed.

Her dark eyes searched his face and as she saw the look of admiration there and something that went deeper than admiration, faint color dyed her face and the hint of a smile crossed her lips. He was so young and so handsome with his tousled reddish brown hair and his deep hazel eyes and the wide mouth with the cleft in the firm chin. There was such an appeal in his eyes that her fear suddenly left her.

Before she could reply Damont intervened. "Mademoiselle, don't be overcome by that heartbreaking appeal," he said and he smiled ingratiatingly. "It's too bad there aren't two of you, for he's doomed to disappointment. I hold the number of your ticket, so by the rules of the Company, you belong to me. I shall try to see that you'll never be sorry that I won you."

Though his lips smiled, there was something in his pale eyes that made Elise uneasy. There was a quality about the man that inspired an instinctive fear in her, the cold ruthlessness and heartless scheming. She met his gaze with a lift of her head and a flash of her eyes and held it.

"Monsieur, I don't belong to you nor to any other man. I have no intention of marrying either one of you." Her voice was firm and she met his eyes unflinchingly.

"That's ridiculous," cried the nun angrily. "You've got to marry someone, so you might as well make up your your mind to accept Monsieur Damont."

"I don't have to marry and no one can make me," she retorted. "I didn't ask to come here and be handed out as if I were a slave or a horse or a piece of furniture, and I never expect to marry in this fashion."

"What fashion do you expect, Mademoiselle?" asked the cool voice of Damont.

"What every girl expects who has a shred of decency. To meet a man someday whom she can love and respect and who loves her for what she is; not to be married off to some stranger who wants her just because she's a woman."

"That's not the reason I want you, Mademoiselle," Damont assured her. "When I saw you on board the ship, you stood out from the rest like a rose among a bunch of withered daisies. I want you because you're so beautiful."

"But you don't know anything about me."

"It makes no difference. I'll have plenty of time to find out all about you." And his smile broadened.

"But I don't know anything about you and I don't love you. I never expect to marry any man until I do."

"Love didn't enter into the picture with the others. Why should it with you?"

The color flamed in her face and the fire flashed in her eyes.

"Because I'm not like those others," she informed him. "It's their misfortune that they were part of the night life of Paris. I've lived a clean life, Monsieur, whether you believe it or not."

"Then why were you taken with those others?" he asked with doubt in his voice. This affair wasn't going the way he had planned it and he was beginning to be uncomfortable in the stare of her scornful eyes.

"I was on my way home from an errand of mercy to a dying woman when two ruffians seized me and took me to the house where they were."

"Enough of this," the nun interposed. "You've got to marry whether you want to or not. There's no such thing as an unmarried girl here."

"There'll be one from now on, until I can get them to send me back to Paris," Elise stated firmly.

Damont smiled. "That won't be possible, Mademoiselle. The ship has gone and it isn't likely that the

Company would bother itself about one stubborn girl when there are so many men who would be willing to give her every comfort here that a woman could want. You'll have to stay here unless your family could send you the money for a return passage."

"I have no family," she admitted.

"Then stop being stubborn," the nun advised. "What will you do if you don't marry? You have no money and no place to go."

"I — I — don't know," she faltered, her voice quavering.

Damont's mind was working rapidly. The very fact that Elise had refused to marry him made him determined to have her. The more he saw her, the more he desired her. He was determined to make the pursuit of her the main object of his life. He had known many women and had loved many in his checkered career, but none of them had possessed the unusual charm that this girl possessed. Though he had been in her presence but a few moments, he recognized something about her which set her apart from all those others. The very inability on his part to solve the enigma of that difference made her more alluring to him.

He realized that there was no use arguing the matter with her now, for he knew from the lift of that firm little chin and the spark in her eyes, that she had meant what she said. She would have neither of them just now.

"Perhaps something can be arranged for Mademoiselle," he said finally. "Old Madame Romain is alone and needs someone to help her. Perhaps Mademoiselle would care to stay with her until she can decide what she wants to do."

His crafty mind hit at once upon what he thought would be the one means of winning her. This was the thought that he would make himself indispensable to her. If he could prove a real friend in time of need, then perhaps in time she would come to love him. He had had success with so many others, how could he fail with this girl?

"Would you care to stay with Madame Romain for a while until you can make some other arrangement?" he asked.

She smiled a tremulous smile. "What else can I do?"

He turned to the nun. "If you'd be good enough to keep Mademoiselle until tomorrow I will see Madame Romain."

The nun agreed and he turned to go. "Until tomorrow, Mademoiselle," he said. "Come, my friend," he said to Chenier who had stood silent during this conversation.

Andre Chenier approached Elise and said in low tones, "Mademoiselle, I'm sorry I misjudged you. Will you forgive me?"

"Of course," she replied, touched by the humility which she could perceive was entirely new to him.

"May I be your friend and may I see you sometime? You'll be needing friends here in New Orleans."

She knew that his words were only too true. She would indeed be needing friends. She smiled. "Yes, Monsieur, and thanks for your offer of friendship. I appreciate it and I shall value it."

He turned toward Damont waiting by the door and his humility suddenly left him. "You watch your step, my fine friend," he challenged defiantly. "Don't try any of your tricks or you'll be sorry. If you harm a hair of her head, you'll be wearing satin for the last time."

CHAPTER 5

When the door had closed behind the two men, the nun turned hostile eyes upon Elise.

"Since Monsieur requested it, you may stay here until tomorrow, but if he doesn't find a place for you, you needn't expect us to keep you here. We have no such intentions. If you can't make up your mind to do as the others and get yourself a good husband, you'll have to look out for yourself."

Elise pressed her lips together to keep back the retort which she felt slipping through them; then said quietly, "I understand. Thank you for letting me stay here until tomorrow."

There was nothing for her to do but wait for the next day. She remained in her room most of the time reading her Bible or sitting by the open window looking out into the brick-paved patio. Again she wondered as she had so many times why God had allowed this to happen to her; but she knew that though she couldn't understand, there was a reason for everything that had happened and that it all fitted into the plan of God for her life. Somewhere at the end of this strange path there would be joy and peace. It was well for her that she could not see what lay between her and the end of this strange path.

Outside the building they had left, the two men paused for a moment and eyed each other. There was a spark of belligerence in Andre Chenier's eyes.

"Just what is your little game?" he demanded. "I know you're not just trying to be kind to Mademoiselle. You're hatching up some scheme and she's going to be led into a trap — a trap that'll keep her until she's willing to marry you. But it won't work. I'm warning you. I'm going to fight you every step of the way for her love, but I'll fight fair. You'd better do the same! Do you get what I mean?"

A twisted smile spread across the thin lips of Andre Damont. His voice was calm, but the look in his eyes was not pleasant. "I think I do, my hot-headed friend. Is there anything else you'd like to warn me of before we part?"

"Yes," retorted Chenier. "I'm going to watch every move you make. Don't you dare try to force that girl to marry you. If you do, she'll be a widow before she has a honeymoon."

He turned upon his heel and left Damont standing there looking after him. There was a venomous gleam in Damont's eyes and his thoughts were rapidly running toward evil: *I'll have to get rid of that hot-headed upstart sooner or later and the sooner the better. I'll have to be careful, though, or I'll do myself more harm than good.* He turned and sauntered in the direction of his office.

This period between the years 1722 and 1727 was one of the most turbulent and trying intervals in the history of the settlement which was destined to be the great city of New Orleans. People from every walk of life had been lured from their homes in Europe to the Louisiana territory by the fabulous stories of John Law and his Mississippi Company. They searched for riches and luxury, but found only poverty, hardships and death. The dregs of society became stranded here, and they brought a period of lawlessness and low morality with which the better class of immigrants found it difficult to cope.

Bienville, the founder of the settlement, had been restored to power and the seat of government of the Louisianan territory had been moved to New Orleans, but the embryo government found it impossible to keep law and order as it should be kept.

Drinking and gambling were the order of the day. Duelling was so frequent that it could almost be termed a pastime. Street brawls not infrequently ended in murder. Among the most reckless and lawless were the *coureurs de hois.* They followed the Indians in their hunting expeditions, bought their furs for a few trinkets and then sold them at a huge profit, shipping many of them to Europe. They grew rich and more reckless as time passed. They also acted as guides to the settlers. They knew the Indians well and many of them had Indian wives.

Of this group, Andre Chenier was perhaps the most daring as well as the most wealthy. Though reckless and adventurous, he did not drink as most of the others did. Perhaps it was because he realized the necessity of keeping a clear head when he lived a life of danger such as his. And in a day when morals were at such low ebb, he had scorned to take an Indian for a wife. He couldn't have told the reason why, but now that he had seen Elise, he was glad that there would be no hindrance to his wooing of her, for he was determined to begin to see her at the earliest opportunity.

Andre Damont was one of the officers of the Mississippi Company. He had come over to the colony at the beginning of the "Mississippi Bubble," as the venture was called. When the truth became known to those who had been duped by John Law's myths about the great wealth to be had in the colony, he had remained even after the bubble had burst. He had become quite a friend of the governor and had influence in the colony. He also had ambitions. This new land offered opportunities to the man who had brains and initiative and a lust for power. Damont had all of these. He and Andre Chenier had become acquainted when he first came to the colony, but they had never liked each other.

He had been attracted to Rosalie Allain but he had no desire to marry her, even if she had not already had a husband. But when he saw Elise, there sprang a new desire within him. He was amazed at himself that he should want a girl of this type, for he thought her like the others who had come over with her. He decided to try marriage even though it might prove disappointing, so he had arranged to get the ticket and to have Elise left until the last. After that brief interview with her he recognized something in her which baffled yet attracted him still more. He was determined to win her, if not by fair means, then by some other way.

He remembered Madame Romain, and his quick mind had hit upon a scheme that might eventually bring him success. If he could persuade or pay the old lady to keep the girl, he could see her as often as he pleased and Rosalie would not be any the wiser. He didn't want her jealousy to interfere with his plan before it had succeeded. He would prove such a friend and benefactor to Elise that she would grow to love him. He felt sure of his power to attract her and felt much pleased with himself as he made his way to Madame Romain's small cottage.

The old lady was crippled and almost blind and dependent upon an Indian maid for her housework. She and her husband had come over in the early days of the Mississippi Company and the husband had been killed in an accident. Fortunately for the old lady they had built the cottage and he had saved a little money, but now that was almost gone.

Damont told her about Elise and pictured to her all the advantages of having the girl live with her and she had finally given a grudging consent to take her in and see how the plan worked. Damont left, feeling satisfied that she would be glad to keep Elise. He would see that she was satisfied, if he had to pay her to keep the girl.

Elise greeted him hopefully as she came into the room where he was waiting for her. She had prayed earnestly that this Madame Romain would take her in. The future looked dark indeed but she was determined not to let fear overwhelm her. She would trust the Lord to keep His word and to provide for all her need.

Damont answered her greeting with what he hoped was a disarming smile. "I have good news for you," he said. "Madame Romain will be glad to give you a home as long as you care to stay with her." This was not the truth, but a lie passed his lips easily when it was to his advantage.

"Oh, that is good news!" Elise exclaimed. "How can I ever thank you for doing this for me?"

"By letting me see you occasionally and by remembering that I shall always be ready to serve you whenever you'll let me."

She smiled. "That would be a small thing to do for all you're doing for me."

As they walked along the wooden banquettes on the narrow streets, Damont pointed out the places of importance.

"That building over there," he remarked, "is the office of the Company of the West." It was a rather imposing structure with a wide stairway leading to a big oak door. The windows of the building were covered with thin cheesecloth, as most of the windows in the better homes were, to keep out the hordes of mosquitoes which swarmed over the city as the wind blew them in from the swamps.

They passed the parish church with its squat towers and the governor's house with its white plastered walls and wide pillared galleries. Negro women with bright-colored tignons wrapped tightly about their heads ambled by, calling out their wares in a sing-song voice. "Bon petite calas. Tout chauds!"

Housewives hurried by, followed by slaves carrying baskets on their way to the Market Place. In the distance they could hear the babel of voices among the stalls facing the open parade ground as vendors in the market proclaimed the excellency of their products. Hunters passed them with their early morning kill hanging over their shoulders — rabbits, squirrels, and one of them even carried a small deer. There would be venison on sale this morning at the market.

"You'll find this quite different from Paris," remarked Damont as they continued on their way. "I hope, though, that life will not be too dull for you. We have occasional parties and balls, although they may not compare with the ones you've attended in Paris."

"I've never had time for many parties, Monsieur, and I've never attended a ball, so I'm afraid I wouldn't be able to compare them."

His eyes widened in surprise but he said nothing. He had forgotten for the moment who she was and why she had come here. He had forgotten that likely there was no place for balls or parties in the class to which she belonged in Paris. The poor of Paris had little time for parties, but somehow, he couldn't picture her as belonging to the poorer element of a slum-crowded city. Her lovely face, her poise, her quiet dignity, the slender white hands, and that clear, steady gaze marked her as belonging to another class entirely. Some day he'd find out all about her; but no matter who she was or what she was, he wanted her and he meant to have her.

They came at last to Madame Romain's cottage. It was isolated from the other houses on the street being separated by a small thicket. It was of rough cypress boards which had once been white-washed, but the white had long since peeled off in spots, leaving a grayish blotched exterior that gave it a drab and dilapidated appearance. Elise's heart sank as she saw the house. It was near the Rampart, on the outskirts of the town, and surrounded by a little yard which had once grown flowers but which was now covered with a rank growth of weeds.

The small front room which they entered was even more drab than the outside and unspeakably dirty and disordered. Madame Romain greeted them sourly and invited them to sit down. Elise wondered how she would be able to endure life here. A great lump rose in her throat. This was so different from the neat little rooms which she had called home after her mother had died.

"I hope that you and Mademoiselle will become friends," Damont said. He felt the depressing effect of the house and he could see the shadow that came over Elise's face as her eyes took in the cluttered room.

"H'm. Yes," Madame emitted unsmilingly.

"I'm sure we shall," Elise said brightly. "I'm so grateful to you, Madame, for letting me stay here. I shall do all in my power to show you how much I appreciate it."

"There'll be plenty for you to do if you'll do it," retorted Madame, but her voice lost some of its harshness. Her dim eyes rested upon the girl's face and the grim lines of her own face softened somewhat. "This place is filthy. That girl I hire doesn't even try to keep it clean. But I don't care much what becomes of it or of me. Life isn't worth living anyway."

Damont left, promising to come back the next day. For some reason which he couldn't explain but which caused him no little annoyance, he couldn't face that forced cheerfulness of Elise which was belied by the look of helplessness and pain upon her face and in her deep brown eyes.

"Where's your clothes?" Madame asked when he had left.

"I haven't any," Elise told her. "They're all back in my room in Paris."

"What're they doing back there and you over here without them? I don't like this business. Did you have to run away because you killed somebody or stole something?"

"Didn't Monsieur Damont tell you why I'm here?" Elise asked.

"No, He only said you were in trouble and needed a home for a while and said if I'd take you in, he'd see that I got paid for my trouble. But I shouldn't have believed him. I shouldn't believe anyone connected with that lying Company. If we hadn't listened to their lies about this place, my Joseph and I would be happy back home in France. What did you run away from?"

"I didn't run away from anything," Elise said with a little tremor in her voice. "I was taken prisoner and brought here with the girls who were brought as wives for the colonists."

"Then why didn't you marry like the rest of them did?" the old lady queried.

"Because I believe that marriage is something sacred and I refused to be handed out to some man I'd never seen before. I don't believe people should marry unless they love each other."

"That's right," agreed the old lady with a sigh. "My

Joseph and I loved each other and we were so happy together. Now it's all over and I've nothing to live for." A tear fell from her eyes and her lips quivered as she struggled to keep back the tears.

Impulsively Elise put an arm around her. "Dear Madame, I know what it is to have everyone that you love taken from you. I know what it is to fight back the tears when it seems that they must come in spite of everything. But there is something to live for or God wouldn't leave you here. He'll bring peace to your heart even if it is broken, just as He has to mine."

"God!" It was a scornful ejaculation. "What does He care about the likes of me? I don't even think about Him any more. I used to when I had my Joseph. We used to go to church every morning and say our beads together, but what did it get us? He got killed and I'm left all crippled and going blind."

"But He still loves you, even though you never think of Him," the girl said softly with her arm still about the old woman.

"Then why don't He show it?

"Perhaps He sent me here so that I could show you how much He loves you."

She jerked herself from Elise's embrace and retorted, "It's too late to show me anything. I don't want to be shown."

She got stiffly to her feet. "Come on and I'll show you where you're to sleep," and she led the way to the back of the house.

The room Elise was to occupy was little more than a big closet. It had a cot and one small window, a shelf on the wall with a cracked mirror over it and a few pegs upon the opposite wall. It was even more depressing than the living room but Elise grimly determined not to be depressed. Some way, somehow, this dark pathway would lead to the light. It must.

God's words were true and she was determined to trust that word.

"This isn't much but it's the best I've got," the old lady said.

"I'm grateful for it," Elise assured her. "Now if you'll show me where things are, I'll start to work and get the place all cleaned up. I'll have everything just as clean as you'd like it to be, in no time at all."

"Don't you want to rest first?" asked Madame in surprise.

"No indeed. I've done nothing but rest since I got on board that ship. I'll enjoy getting a broom in my hands and doing some real work for a change.

"I believe I'm going to like you after all," the old lady reluctantly admitted.

CHAPTER 6

The task of cleaning up the cottage was more than Elise had anticipated. The place was unspeakably dirty. The Indian maid had known that Madame couldn't see very well and she had let the dirt pile up. She was just a part-time servant and got through with her work as soon as she could, not caring how much she neglected.

By noon Elise was glad to rest for a while. She was not only tired but very hungry. Madame admitted that she was hungry also but she said she didn't know whether there was any food in the house or not. Elise searched the untidy kitchen which she hadn't yet reached with her mop and broom and she found some meal, a crock of milk and some stale bread. She lighted a fire in the stove and made some mush; then toasted the bread. When Madame hobbled into the kitchen to see what she was doing, she had already set the table and had the simple meal ready. She took her place at the table while Elise held her chair for her. Then the girl sat down and, without asking permission, asked the Lord's blessing upon the food.

"Why did you do that?" Madame asked querulously.

"I always thank God for providing the food I eat,"

she replied. "I never thought to ask you. I'm sorry if I offended."

"Why thank God for this stuff?" Madame retorted.

"Because all that we have comes from Him. I think this tastes pretty good. Don't you?" She smiled to herself as Madame grunted an assent; for the old lady was eating the mush and milk and crisp toast as if she were enjoying it immensely. In reality it was the most tasty food she had had in a long time.

That afternoon when the Indian maid came, Madame informed her that her services were no longer needed. The girl took a quick look about the house and noted the transformation that had taken place; then her baleful glance rested upon Elise's flushed and perspiring face. Elise knew when the girl had left that she had made an enemy.

That night when Elise finally got into bed she was too tired to mind the cobwebs which still hung from the ceiling of her room. She had managed to wash and iron the sheets and to clean the rest of the house, but her own small room she decided to leave for another day.

The next morning she was up long before Madame wakened. She got out her Bible and read several chapters; then she went outside to take a look at the yard. Those weeds would have to be cut down before she could do anything with the garden, she decided, but she wondered how that was to be done. It would take a stronger arm and back than she possessed and she knew that Madame had no money with which to hire a man to clean the place. But she wanted flowers and she wanted the place to be as attractive as possible. If this was to be her home for even a short while, she couldn't face the unhealthy look of the weed-infested garden.

While she was standing there wondering what to do, someone approached from the town. She saw that it was Andre Chenier. His bronze hair was uncovered and was ruffled by the breeze which came from the river. His eyes were alight with a look that brought a swift surge of color to her face. He was even more good looking today, with the brown leggings, the cream colored shirt open at the throat and the broad smile upon his lips. His belligerence had left him and good humor had taken its place, and the difference made him far more attractive.

"Good morning, Mademoiselle," he said as he stopped outside the gate. "You're up early."

She gave him an answering smile. "I always get up early. I like the early morning better than any part of the day. I was just looking over the yard."

"Looks more like a wilderness than a garden. And the house isn't any palace, is it?" he remarked as he gazed at the dilapidated cottage and weed-choked yard.

"No. But I'm thankful for it and grateful to Madame for taking me in. The garden will look better when I get these weeds cleared out and some flowers planted."

"You could never cut these weeds down. They're young trees."

"That's what I was thinking when you came."

"Then I came just in time," and he smiled again. "If you want to plant flowers, you shall plant them. I'm just the fellow who can get rid of those weeds in no time at all."

"O Monsieur!" she protested. "I could never let you do that!"

"Why not? This will be play for me. When a fellow has had to cut a trail through a wilderness as I've had to do many times, cutting down a few weeds won't amount to anything. It'll be fun."

"But — but — Monsieur —"

"But nothing. Didn't I tell you that I'd be your friend and that you could call upon me when you needed a friend? You just wait until I get my tools and I'll have the work all done so soon that you'll be surprised."

While he went down the street with long swinging strides she sat upon the low step and waited for him. In spite of herself she felt attracted to him. She was glad that he wanted to be her friend. She mentally compared him with Damont. His clear gaze, his warm friendly smile, everything about him expressed frankness. His very impetuosity on the day she first met him revealed a quality which she found more to be commended than condemned. Damont's manner somehow chilled her even when he was befriending her. There was nothing frank about him. She felt that there was a ruthlessness beneath that outward charm which he strove to exercise, that would crush anything or anyone that stood in the way of his desires.

In less time than she had thought possible Chenier returned. He carried a shovel, axe and hoe and was soon at work getting rid of the weeds. While he cut them down or dug them up, she helped as much as he would let her. She gathered the smaller ones into piles to be burned, while he carried the larger ones to the back corner of the yard. As they worked they talked. He told her something of his life here and of his trips through the forests and his trade with the Indians. She told him of her life in Paris, of her happy home which had been wrecked by the death of her parents, and then of her work in the city as a salesgirl in one of the shops.

They forgot time until the raucous voice of Madame called from the porch.

"What are you doing out there?" she wanted to know.

"We're clearing away the weeds, so you can have a pretty flower garden," Elise told her as she went to where the old lady stood.

"Where did you get that fellow and who's going to pay him for his work?" demanded Madame.

Chenier approached and Elise introduced him. "This is Monsieur Chenier, Madame Romain. And he's not charging us anything for this work."

"Why not?"

"Because he's a friend and wants to help."

"I wonder how many more men saw that you were in trouble and wanted to help. I want my breakfast. It's way past time for it."

"I'll come and fix it now," Elise told her. She excused herself to Chenier and went inside. She tried to forget the old lady's harsh words and insinuations, but they stung and hurt her.

She discovered that there was coffee and the end of a slab of bacon in the cupboard so she built the fire and started the water boiling for the coffee. It wasn't long before she had cooked the bacon, in thin, crisp slices and had toasted the bread and made the coffee. The aroma filled the small kitchen and as Madame hobbled in at her summons, there was a more pleasant look on her face.

"What's this other plate for?" she asked as she noted that Elise had set the table for three.

"I thought perhaps you'd like to ask Monsieur Chenier in to breakfast. Don't you think he would appreciate being asked? He's been working hard and I'm sure he hasn't had his breakfast yet."

"What will Monsieur Damont say to your asking this fellow in?"

"Why should he say anything?" asked Elise in surprise.

"If he's going to pay me for your keep, what will he say when he finds that this other fellow is eating meals here?"

Elise's voice took on a sharper edge as she said, "Monsieur Damont isn't going to pay for my keep,

Madame. I think I'm earning it at present. I'm trying to anyway. And just as soon as I can find work, I shall pay you myself."

"Then what'll I do without you?" cried Madame. "I mean who will look after me while you're at work?"

Elise smiled. She put an arm around Madame's shoulder and said, "Don't worry about that until the time comes. I shall see that you're taken care of. Now shall I invite Monsieur in to breakfast?"

"Oh, I suppose so," Madame grudgingly consented.

Elise hastened outside to the far corner of the yard where Chenier was working.

"Madame invites you to have breakfast with us," she told him. "We don't have much to offer, but we shall be glad to share it with you."

"I accept with pleasure," he replied as he gave a mock bow. "I'm as hungry as a wolf and the smell of that bacon gave me an added appetite. I'm sure it wasn't Madame's thoughtfulness that made her invite me, though," he added as they went toward the house.

Madame was waiting impatiently for them as they took their places at the table. Before the old lady could help herself to the food, Elise bowed her head and returned thanks in a few simple words. As she raised her head Madame was glaring at her angrily.

"Do I have to wait for that every time we sit down to eat?" she asked testily.

"No, Madame," the girl replied quietly, "You may go ahead and eat if you wish. But I shall return thanks before I eat," she added with a note of firmness in her voice.

Madame lapsed into an angry silence. When she had finished eating, she came out of her silence long enough to remark, "You'll have to go to market if we are to have anything to eat today."

"I'll go as soon as I've finished the dishes," Elise replied. "I suppose I can find the Market Place."

"Of course you can. This street leads straight to the river and you can't miss the Market Place. But you'll have to go right away and do the dishes when you get back. If you wait too long everything will be picked over."

"There'll be venison there today," Chenier remarked. "I saw a hunter on his way to market when I came by there."

"I can't afford venison," Madame snapped. "I'll be glad to get a few eggs or some fish."

"If you'd be kind enough to invite me back to dinner, I'd be glad to get the venison. That is, if Mademoiselle wouldn't mind cooking it."

"I'll pay for my own food," Madame retorted. "When I can't, I'll starve, I suppose. And I'm not running a boarding house."

"Madame, dear, don't say that," Elise begged. She put one small hand over the old lady's withered one on the table. "Monsieur has been so kind in helping us get rid of those weeds. We'll be repaying him for what he has done by letting him eat some of my cooking. I can make a stew that will make your mouth water just to smell it."

"We'll be repaying him by letting him buy our meat. How do you figure that out?" The voice was harsh but her withered old face softened just a trifle. The touch of Elise's hand upon hers had done something to her. It was the first touch of tenderness she had felt since her beloved Joseph had left her.

Elise laughed and said, "We'll just call it give and take. He gave us help when we needed it and we invited him to breakfast. He'll get the venison and we'll let him eat the best dinner he's had in a long time. Isn't that a fair exchange?"

Chenier grinned at the frustrated look on the old lady's face.

"Girl, you've got a way with you," she said. "I pity the man who marries you. You'll twist him around your finger and he'll like it. Go and get the venison before it's all gone," and she shoved back her chair and hobbled from the room.

After Elise had given Andre a clean towel and he had washed his face and hands, they left the house. They walked along the tree-shaded Esplanade past high-pillared houses where the more prosperous lived. Soon they were on the narrow streets which were already swarming with children playing in front of low doorsteps of hewn logs. Some housewives were busy scrubbing the steps, while others were hurrying down to the Market Place, their long skirts switching about their ankles and kicking up the dust as they walked. The sing-song chant of the black vendors carrying their trays of cakes or candies could be heard as they approached. "Pralines pistache! Pralines pecones!" they cried in high melodious voices. "Belle de figues!"

"That old witch is going to make life miserable for you," Chenier commented. "She has as much venom as a water moccasin."

"She really hasn't, but sorrow has made her bitter. She has lost everything that made her life worth living. She's old and lonely and she feels that she has no one to love her."

"Who could love an old crone like her?"

"God loves her and I shall try to make her understand and to get her to love Him."

"How will you do that? It'll be a big job to get her to love anything or anybody."

"I shall try to be so kind and thoughtful of her that perhaps she will come to love Him through me."

"That ought not to be hard. I could love anyone

through you." The look that went with the words brought the color flooding her face.

"Please, Monsieur, we're to be friends. Remember? Let's not forget that."

"I'm not forgetting and I won't annoy you, I promise you. But that won't stop me from loving you. When I first saw you on the boat I fell in love with you. I know myself well enough to know that I shall always love you."

"That's not love, Monsieur," she said seriously. "You may have been attracted by my face because — well, because there were so few girls here, but that isn't love. Love goes much deeper than physical attraction."

"I understand," he replied gravely. "And that's why I know that the love I have for you is the kind of love you're talking about."

She gave him a surprised glance, then swiftly averted her gaze. She was provoked with herself at the sudden fluttering of her heart.

"Something has happened to me since I met you," he continued, "something that surprises me and bewilders me. You see, I never respected women before I met you. The only girls I ever came in contact with were just cheap little cheats who'd stoop to anything to possess a few trinkets or a little money. Even when I thought you were like the others, I wanted to marry you. Though I'm sure you won't be flattered by what I'm saying, you are the only girl I ever wanted to marry. Now that I realize how different you are from anyone I've ever known, that makes me want you all the more."

She was silent, trying to control the wild beating of her heart. This was a different man from the one she had met at the home of the nuns and there was something about him which stirred her as she had never been stirred before. It annoyed her, for she had been so determined to keep coolly indifferent to anyone who was not a Christian.

"I want to apologize for the way I acted the other day," he said. "I was an impetuous fool. I thought of course you were here looking for a husband and I was egotistical enough to believe that you'd consider what I had to offer you as something worthwhile. Judging by your remark about what real love is, I'm afraid that I don't have anything to offer you. Nothing, that is, but money."

"You have offered me something that I shall treasure, Monsieur. That is your friendship. You've already proved to me how valuable that is by what you did this morning," and she smiled into his serious face.

"If we're to be friends, won't you call me Andre?" he replied. "Monsieur sounds so stiff and formal."

"I'll think about it," she promised. "You and Monsieur Damont have the same given name, haven't you?"

"Yes, I'm sorry to say," he said as a shadow crossed his face.

She hastened to change the subject. They had encountered several Indians making their way to the Market Place with wares to sell. Some of them had baskets, others had beaded work, while one big fellow carried a string of squirrels over his shoulder.

"Are the Indians allowed to come and go as they please?" she asked. "I thought it would be dangerous to the colonists to allow them to come into town whenever they wished."

"These are friendly Indians," he told her. "They belong to the *Chouachas.* Their settlement is just above the city. But if real trouble ever comes, I'm afraid they'll take sides with their own people against the whites. I can't much blame them for hating us. We've come to their land and robbed and plundered and killed them when they trusted us. Now we're paying the penalty for what the early explorers did. There's always danger that they may rise against us and wipe us all out. They could, if they could only get together, but they're always fighting each other."

They had reached the Market Place and she saw that it was swarming with people. There was a confusion of sound as purchasers haggled over the prices of meat and fruit and vegetables. German and French mingled in discordant notes with the low guttural tones of the Indian dialect. Elise was surprised to note that many of the housewives who were accompanied by their slaves were dressed in silk, having their hair piled high in the latest Paris fashion and wearing jeweled pins and glittering diamonds upon their white hands. Though the colony was still young, there was wealth here and love of expensive clothes and jewels just as there was in the land from which they had emigrated.

Elise and Andre soon made their purchases and left. The basket which Elise had brought was piled high with provisions. Chenier carried it and they started back toward the cottage. Just as they crossed the street they came face to face with Damont. He gave them a surprised stare and there flashed in his eyes a faint glimmer of the anger which stirred within him at the sight of these two together.

"Good morning, Monsieur," Elise called to him as he approached. "You can see we have been to market. It's been a new experience for me. I promised Madame Romain that I'd fix her the most tempting meal she has had in a long time."

"If it's going to be that good, I wonder if I might share it," Damont said with a smile. But his eyes did not smile.

"Why — of course —"

"Madame Romain already has one invited guest," Chenier interrupted.

"That's quick work, my friend," Damont's cold voice replied.

"Oh, Monsieur, I'd be glad to have you and I'm sure Madame would be glad also," Elise hastened to say. She could feel the tense situation and she sensed the dislike between the two. "Monsieur Chenier was kind enough to clear Madame's garden of the weeds this morning so that I could plant flowers. He came by while I was wondering how I could get them cleared away. Since he was so kind, I — I wanted to repay him in some small way. Won't you join us this evening, too?"

"Thank you, Mademoiselle, but I'll come some other time, if I may. I think you have quite enough company for this time."

He bowed and passed on. Fury was raging within him. The girl was even more lovely this morning than he had remembered her. And she seemed to be enjoying Chenier's company. He had to admit that the fellow was handsome — in a crude sort of way. And even though she had pretended to be so indifferent to the thought of marriage, he had an idea that money could change her mind. Chenier had plenty of that and this thought made him even more jealous. Chenier was much nearer the girl's age and the very fact of his adventurous life might appeal to her.

He realized, with a sense of futility, that there was nothing he could do to stop Chenier from seeing her. If he should try to do that, it would only make her more interested in him. He would have to find some other means of eliminating Chenier from the scene. In the meantime, he'd keep a closer watch upon Chenier. And he'd try to make himself indispensable to the girl. What a smart idea for Chenier to stroll past the cottage and prove himself the friend in need this morning! Why hadn't he thought of that himself? Even getting his soft hands dirty and bringing out the perspiration upon his silk shirt would have been worth while if it would aid his cause with her.

When he saw how much Chenier wanted her, it but fanned the flame of his own obsession. It was one characteristic of his scheming, ruthless nature to want something which seemed unattainable. The more remote that something seemed, the more he became determined to possess it. It was the desire for power which had kept him here after the Mississippi Company faced failure. His shrewd mind had conceived the idea that one day he would replace Bienville and become head of the Louisiana colony. His plans were just vaguely shaping, but he felt that in the end he'd succeed. Now had come this girl, lovely and unapproachable. Because she held herself aloof she had become more desirable every day since he had first seen her.

"My friend Damont didn't seem very much pleased to find us together," Chenier remarked as they left him.

"I'm sorry if he was angry," she said. "I wouldn't want to hurt him. He's been so kind to me in finding me a place to stay."

"Don't worry. He won't be angry with you. But he'll be furious with me. I may have to kill him yet."

"O Monsieur, don't say that!" she cried.

"Please! 'Andre,' not 'Monsieur,' " he urged playfully.

"Well — Andre, then. But don't talk about killing anyone. If you did that, I wouldn't even call you 'Monsieur.' "

He laughed. "All right, then. I promise you not to kill him. At least not unless I have to. I wouldn't do anything that would cause me to lose your friendship."

The dinner that evening was even more than Chenier had anticipated. After their return from the market, he had finished cleaning up the yard and

Elise had finished cleaning the cottage. When he returned later, he was so immaculately dressed that she was amazed and couldn't help but show it.

"Monsieur! Are you going to a party?"

He laughed rather sheepishly. "I feel like a dressed up monkey in these things," and he cast an eye over his tight black trousers, the white ruffled shirt and plaid waistcoat. "But this is quite an event to me and I wanted to be dressed in keeping with the occasion. Silly of me, wasn't it?" and he gave her a boyish grin that brought a smile to her lips.

"You make me feel terribly dowdy in this much-worn dress. Some day I hope to get another."

Madame was drawn out of her silence by the delicious food and she joined in the conversation with a word now and then. Elise felt well repaid for the work she had had to do in preparing the meal and was encouraged to hope that soon she would be able to break through that wall of bitterness and sorrow and let the light of the love of Christ shine into the old lady's heart.

When Chenier prepared to leave Elise went with him to the gate.

"I want to thank you again for all you've done for me today," she said. "You have been a real friend and I do appreciate it more than I can say."

She gave him her hand and he clasped it in his; then put it to his lips and kissed it. With a murmured goodnight, he left her, walking with graceful swinging strides. As she watched him go into the gathering dusk, mingled emotions stirred within her heart. She remained a long time upon her knees that night, asking for guidance and for strength to face whatever the future might hold. She already sensed the conflict which might come and she wanted to be prepared to meet it, not in her own strength, nor her own will but in God's.

CHAPTER 7

Damont came the next afternoon and brought a bouquet of flowers as well as many packages of seed.

"I thought you might be wanting to get that garden started," he said, "Since you already have a gardener, I won't offer my services, but I'll be glad to help if you need me."

"Thank you so much, but I think I can manage, now that the weeds are all cleared away. I love to work with flowers, but I've never had a garden since my mother died. There is something that perhaps you might be able to help me with," she added after a pause.

"Just name it," he said. He smiled but there was no warmth in his smile. She mentally compared his smile with the smile of the other Andre with the cleft in his chin and the warm friendliness in his hazel eyes.

"I must find something to do, Monsieur," she said. "I wonder if you could suggest where I could look for some kind of work."

"Why worry about finding work? You have a home here with Madame. I'll confess it's no palace, but you may not have to stay here long. Some day some lucky man will give you a better home. I don't need to tell you that I'm hoping to be that lucky man."

She raised a protesting hand. "Monsieur! Please!"

"I know I may seem impetuous and I know that isn't according to the social customs you've been used to, but life here is very different. We men have been so lonely and so starved for the things which only a woman can give — companionship, a home, someone to love. I'm not going to annoy you nor try to force you to accept me, Mademoiselle, but I do ask that you give me a chance to try to win your love. I'm so afraid that someone else might win you and I so desperately want your love."

"I'm not thinking about marrying just now, Monsieur. Please give me time to get adjusted to life here. I haven't yet gotten over the shock of being uprooted and set down in this strange place. And I must find work. I have no clothes and Madame has very little money."

"Won't you let me help you? I have more money than I need. You could call it a loan if you won't accept it any other way."

"How could I ever repay you if I didn't get work and earn money?"

"Let's not worry about that. Let the future take care of that. This is a present emergency."

She shook her head. "That's kind of you, but I couldn't let you do that. I must look for work. I was hoping that perhaps you might suggest something."

"What kind of work can you do?"

"I'm afraid I'm not equipped to do much of anything. That's what's bothering me. I sold dresses in one of the big shops in Paris, but there are no big shops here, are there?"

"No, there are not," he admitted.

"I can cook and sew and do housework. That's the extent of my accomplishments. Not a very promising array, is it?"

"You say you can sew," he said after a time. He wanted to help her but he didn't want her to get to where she wouldn't need his help. "Perhaps you might find a good market for your talent with the wives of our colonists. Though many of them have slaves who do the sewing, there are others who don't have them. I'm sure that the girls who came over with you will need many things. Perhaps they'd be glad to have you sew for them."

"Oh, I hadn't thought of that," she said. "I think it's a wonderful idea. Thank you for suggesting it. I shall start out tomorrow morning and see what I can do."

His busy mind was working out a scheme of his own. "If you'll wait a day or so, I think I can get you a list of names of those who would want your services. I know the people and where they live and it would save you a lot of unnecessary walking."

"That's so very kind of you," she said with a smile. "But won't it put you to too much trouble?"

"Where you're concerned, nothing will ever be too much trouble," he assured her.

The look which went with the words would have brought a thrill to her if it had come from the other Andre, but now it left her cold. He felt her coldness and it angered him. He was making slow progress with her, he realized, but he was willing to bide his time. He wondered what success Chenier was having. No matter what success Chenier had he should never have her, he told himself grimly.

"I shall come back tomorrow," he told her, "and by then I shall have a number of customers for you. I can get others later, but I'm sure you'll have a number to start with."

"I can never thank you enough for what you have done and are doing for me," she said.

"Just let me be your friend and free to serve you

when you need me. Why not call me Andre? If we're to be friends, it will make me much happier if you do. 'Monsieur' sounds so formal."

"Perhaps I may, some day," she promised, "Somehow I can't just now. It sounds foolish, I know, but I just can't."

When he had gone, she went into the garden and began to dig the beds and plant the seeds. While she was at work Chenier came by and stopped at the gate.

"Would you be needing a gardner to help you?" he asked.

She rose from her knees and went to him. She wore a worn and faded apron that belonged to Madame; her hair hung in disordered curls about her flushed face; but to him she had never looked more lovely.

"I think I can manage without your help today," she smiled. "You've already done too much for me."

"I could never do too much for you." His words quickened the throb of her heart. "That's what friends are for, isn't it? To help one another?"

"And what a friend you've been, Monsieur!"

He pointed an admonitory finger at her. "Andre, remember. Not Monsieur."

"Very well, Andre. Would you come in and watch me work or do you have business elsewhere?"

"I shall come in and help whether you need me or not," he stated. "And I've no business just now but that of looking after you. I shall have to make a trip soon to one of the Indian villages but just now I want to help you to become adjusted and to be as happy as possible in this new life. I see you've been shopping," he remarked as she opened one of the seed packages.

"No. Monsieur Damont brought them to me. It was very thoughtful of him, wasn't it?"

Andre ignored the question and said, "Let me help you plant them."

"You've already done so much. If you hadn't cleared the weeds away I couldn't have used the seeds at all. Monsieur Damont has given me an idea for getting work," she continued. "Tomorrow I'm going to begin sewing for some of the women. He's going to get me a list of names and show me where they live. I'm so grateful to him for I do want to get some work. My two dresses are almost worn to shreds. Besides, I must begin to pay Madame for my room and board."

"I think you're more than paying her by what you're doing for her," he said. He didn't say what was on his mind concerning Damont. He knew that there was going to be a subtle war between them for the love of this girl and he wasn't too sure that the war would not end in open conflict.

"What I'm doing won't put food in the cupboard," she told him. "And Madame keeps reminding me that her money is fast giving out."

As they worked they talked. He told her amusing incidents of his dealings with the Indians and she told him more of her early life with her parents. She told him of her experiences on board the ship and of the storm and how frightened the girls were.

"Why weren't you afraid?" he asked.

"Because God has taken the fear of death out of my heart. Those girls knew nothing of the love of God and they had no hope beyond this life. It was natural for them to be afraid."

"The love of God?" echoed Chenier. "I never heard anyone talk about God's love. In fact the only time I've ever heard God mentioned was when some fellow cursed."

"How terrible!" she exclaimed. "How much you have missed."

"I hadn't noticed it," he remarked with a whimsical smile. "What have I missed?"

"The greatest thing in the world. And the most important thing in life. To know the love of God and to know Jesus Christ as your own personal Saviour is something that you need, not only through death and all eternity, but for this life too."

"Do you really believe that there is a life beyond this one?" he asked.

"Why of course. I know there is. Don't you believe that?" Her wide serious eyes were fastened on him.

"I never bothered to think about it," he admitted. "I've been too much occupied with this life to think of what lies beyond. I suppose I didn't want to think about it."

"It's time you should, Andre," she said gently.

His eyes lighted at the sound of his name upon her lips.

"This life is too uncertain," she continued, "for us to go on living without any thought or preparation for eternity. I'm so glad that I found Christ as my Saviour before I came here. I don't know what I would have done during all this time if I hadn't had Jesus Christ to comfort me."

He regarded her gravely; then said, "Now I know why you're so different from anyone I've ever met. You have something that I can't understand, something I've never heard of before. It makes you different."

"If you had that something as I have it, it would make you different too."

"Would it make you care for me, even just a little bit?"

The look and the tones of his voice brought once more the thrill to her heart and the color to her face.

"It would make me very happy," she told him.

"Then tell me more about it and I'll do whatever it takes to get it."

She smiled. "You don't get it that way. It's not something one puts on or gets by just making up his mind that he'll get it, like some material thing. What I'm talking about is salvation through the blood of Christ. You must realize that you're a sinner, doomed to eternal punishment without Christ. For all of us are born with a sinful nature."

"I know that only too well," he admitted. "When you've lived here as long as I have and seen what I've seen, you wonder if there's anything else but sin in the world."

"That's why God sent His Son to die on the Cross for me. You see, when Jesus died on the Cross He paid the penalty for our sin; He took the sin of the whole world in His own person. He shed His blood for our sins because God had decreed that without the shedding of blood there is no remission for sin. When you realize that you're a sinner and really want to be saved from the penalty of sin, you have to come to Him and ask Him for pardon and salvation and He gives you salvation as a free gift. We can't work for it or do penance for it. He did it all for us on the cross."

"Where did you learn all this? I never heard anything like it."

"My mother first told me about it, and then I read it for myself in the Bible. My Bible was the only thing I brought with me when they captured me that night. I hid it in my pocket when I went to see that dying woman. I don't know what I'd do without it."

"How could such a simple thing as you suggest make a person so different? It just doesn't make sense."

"I can't explain it. It's one of God's miracles. I suppose the greatest miracle of all. When we receive salvation and Christ enters our heart we become a new creature. I don't know how He does it; I just know that He does."

"I wish I could believe it as you do," he said with a note of regret in his voice.

"Perhaps one day you will," she replied. "I shall pray that you will."

"You will?" Again there was that warm note in his voice as his eyes rested upon her face. "Thanks for that. It will be the first time anyone has ever prayed for me."

"Have you ever prayed for yourself?" she asked.

"No, I haven't. Who ever heard of a *coureur de bois* praying for anything? He'd be the laughing stock of the whole outfit if he did. We depend upon ourselves!"

"And yet you couldn't even breathe without God," she informed him.

He stared at her in surprise. "How is that?"

"Because He controls the universe. Every breath you draw comes from Him. If He took His hand off your life for a moment, you'd die."

"I wish I could believe," he repeated.

"You will, some day," she affirmed.

When they had finished planting the seeds, it was almost dusk. She was very tired but she was far happier than she had been since the night of her capture. Chenier washed his hands and prepared to leave.

"I'd invite you to dinner," she told him, "but we have nothing but bread and milk. Some day soon I hope we can have more and then I shall be so glad to have you dine with us."

"I won't wait until I'm invited to dinner before I see you again," he said as he left her.

This time as she watched his retreating figure there was a prayer in her heart that the little seed she had sown might one day bring forth fruit in his heart and that he too would be a new creation in Christ.

CHAPTER 8

Annette was one of the first customers Elise had. She had married Monsieur Boudreaux and lived on the Bayou. Monseiur Boudreaux had a little vegetable garden and a few cows. He was a carpenter. When Elise went to their home she found Annette working in the garden. She was surprised and pleased at the change she saw in the girl, even in the few short days since she had last seen her. Her face was flushed from the exercise and her hair was hanging loosely about her face, but the hard bitter lines were gone and the sneer from her lips. In her eyes there was no longer the cynicism that Elise had seen there so often. The possession of a home and someone to provide for her had done much to change her.

"This is a joke," was her greeting when Elise called a good morning to her. "You working for me. Who'd ever have guessed it?"

"We never can tell what a day may bring forth," Elise replied. "How do you like working in the garden? I've just finished planting some flowers in Madame's garden."

"Strange to say, I do like it," Annette admitted as she shook the dirt off her dress and wiped her hands. "Come on in the house and we'll see what we can do about the sewing. Monsieur Damont seems much interested in your welfare," she added wryly. There was a hint of the old sarcasm in her voice.

"He's been very kind." Elise told her. "When I said I wanted to get some sewing he offered to help me find it. I never thought I'd be coming here first."

"My husband knows Monsieur. He has done a lot of work for Monsieur and for the Company. Helped to build his house and the office building. Why bother about getting sewing? Why don't you go ahead and marry the man and let him work for you? It's much better than having to look out for yourself."

"For the same reason I didn't marry him that first day," Elise replied. "I don't love him."

"Nonsense. All that moonlight and romance stuff is good enough, but for all practical purposes it won't work. Look at me. I didn't love the fellow I married, but I took him. And whether you believe it or not, it's working out better than I would have expected. Henri is kind to me and he's a good provider. What else could anyone like me ask for? I like him well enough and we get along fairly well together. Anyway, it's better than what I left back in Paris," and the hard gleam flashed for a moment in her dark eyes.

"You really look happy and I'm so glad. It has taken away some of the bitterness, hasn't it?"

"Yes, it has," Annette admitted. "It's so good to have a home and someone who can be a companion and not a beast like those others back in Paris."

"I was praying that you'd find happiness and that the bitterness would leave," Elise said as her eyes rested upon Annette's flushed face.

"It's a wonder you'd even want to speak to me, much less pray for me, after the way I treated you," Annette remarked as she led the way into the house.

The house was small but clean and comfortable. It

was built of cypress but it had been whitewashed recently and the inside walls were tinted and looked fresh and attractive. There were crisp curtains at the windows to hide the netting, and upon the floor were woven rugs. The small room looked quite inviting.

"It looks lovely," Elise told her as they entered and Annette invited her to sit down.

"I've worked like fury to get it all cleaned up. I just washed and ironed the curtains yesterday. They were a sight. A man can't keep the place looking decent and those lazy Indian maids don't ever seem to see the dirt until they can't walk over it."

They discussed the sewing for a while. Annette needed everything and she couldn't sew. The prices in the few shops were quite high for anyone who had to be outfitted all at once. Annette reminded her that all the other newly-weds would be in the same situation she was in. As the day passed, Elise found it to be true. By the time she got home that evening she had more work on hand than she had hoped for.

She had met Claire in the course of her visits and was pleased to see that Claire also seemed happier than she had ever hoped to be. She tried to talk to Claire about the Lord before she left her, but Claire wasn't inclined to listen.

"I won't bother you, dear," Elise told her when she saw the girl's indifference, "but you told me on board the ship that you wanted me to tell you more about salvation."

"Yes, I know I did," Claire admitted, "but things are different now. Tony doesn't bother with religion at all and I don't think it would do any good just now for me to get interested in it."

"But I'm not talking about religion, Claire. I wanted to talk to you about Jesus and about accepting Him as your Saviour."

Claire shrugged. "But I'm not interested now. Some other time, maybe, but not now."

"All right. I won't bore you if you're not interested. But you remember the storm, don't you?"

"Of course. Could I ever forget it? I never was so frightened in my life."

"How do you know there won't be something even worse than a storm to frighten you here?" Elise asked her. "Indian massacres, for instance. They have happened before and they could happen again."

"Are you trying to frighten me?" Claire asked irritably.

"No, dear. I'm just reminding you how uncertain life is. It's such a comfort to know that no matter what the future holds, we need not be afraid."

"I'm not thinking about the future," the girl informed her. "I'm living in the present and it's turning out much better than I ever thought it would. Tony is good to me and I believe I'm in love with him. I have a home and don't have to go out to sell myself for liquor to give that old father of mine. Don't try to upset me by bringing up unpleasant thoughts about the future."

As Elise went home that evening, a sense of loneliness and disappointment swept over her. She was afraid that she had approached Claire in the wrong way. In all this settlement there appeared to be no one with whom she could have fellowship in the Lord. People seemed to have forgotten that He existed or if they ever thought of Him at all, they refused to give Him any place in their lives. There was a church, it was true, and each morning the faithful went there to early mass and knelt before the altar with their beads, but their worship seemed to be mockery. It was all so mechanical and formal. It was the same all over the world, she thought sadly. Men had the form of godliness but denied the power thereof. It was the same even in Paul's day. How the heart of the great apostle must have ached over this same situation. How the heart of God must ache over indifferent, lost humanity!

She arose with the dawn and worked late into the night to keep up with her work. Even then, the sewing began to pile up and her customers became impatient for their work. She found the days too short for what she had to do. There was the cooking and housecleaning, the marketing and the garden work, washing and ironing as well as her sewing. When she received her first pay for her sewing she went on a small shopping spree. She bought material for a dress for herself, though she wondered when she was ever going to find time to make it. She then went to the market and bought a few of the things that she knew Madame liked but which she had refused to buy for fear that the money would give out.

When she came home with her purchases, she laid the marketing on the kitchen table and called to Madame. "Come and see what we're going to have for dinner," she said. "There's a nice fat rabbit and some rice and peas and a 'sabotin.' And we're going to have pineapple for dessert."

"Where did the money come from for all of this?" Madame wanted to know. She had been cross with Elise about the marketing ever since the girl had told her that she would not allow Damont to pay for her board.

"I got paid today for some of my sewing," Elise told her. "I shall be getting more from now on. I thought we'd celebrate, so I got some of the things you like."

"What did you buy for yourself?" Madame asked.

"A few yards of print for a dress. I'll soon wear out the two I have."

"You shouldn't have spent so much money on food." Madame's voice was less harsh.

"But I wanted you to have something you liked. You've been so good to me that I wanted to do something nice for you."

Madame's dim eyes looked at her solemnly, and there was a quaver in her voice as she said, "I haven't been nice to you at all, and you know it. What makes you so good to me when I'm so cross with you?"

Elise put an arm around the thin shoulders. "Because I love you and because I know how you've suffered. You see, I too have suffered and I know just how it feels."

Tears welled up in the dim eyes and trickled down the withered cheeks. "No one has ever said that to me before," she spoke hesitatingly. "No one since my Joseph died. How can you love me when I've been so mean to you?"

Elise rejoiced over the tears, for she realized that at last that wall of bitterness and hate around the old lady's heart was melting.

"I love you because my Lord loves you," she said gently. "Some day when you come to love Him as I do, you'll understand. If it hadn't been for His sustaining power in my life, I'd have been just as bitter as you've been and just as full of despair, for I have no one to love me, either, and I know what loneliness and heartache are."

The old lady cried softly while the girl's arms enveloped her; then she raised her head and wiped her eyes with the back of her hand. There was a twinkle in her eyes that gleamed through the tears.

"You can't say that you have no one to love you when two fine young men are practically sitting on the doorstep waiting for you to say the word and marry one of them."

Elise laughed. "The kind of love that they offer

isn't what I'm looking for just now. Perhaps some day the right man will come along, but until then let's get busy with dinner or we'll both be starving."

That evening, for the first time, there was no irritable grunt or mumbled complaint when Elise bowed her head and returned thanks before they ate. Later, as she was in her room sewing, the old lady hobbled in. Elise hastened to give her the only chair while she sat upon the cot.

"I've been thinking a lot about what you said," Madame began. "Tell me about the love of God. If it made you what you are and kept you from being as miserable as I've been since my Joseph died, maybe it can do something for me. But I have my doubts."

"I don't. I know it will bring peace to your heart that you've never known before."

Elise began to tell her as simply as she could of the love of God, beginning with the verse that contains the whole theme of salvation in a few lines, "For God so loved the world that He gave his only begotten Son, that whosoever believeth in Him should not perish, but have everlasting life." From there she gave her the plan of salvation, so simple, yet so wonderful and beyond human understanding. Then she gave her own testimony, of how God had sustained and comforted her when she had lost everything that made life happy for her, of how He had brought her through trying experiences until this present time.

The old lady's voice was strangely soft as she spoke. "It sounds so wonderful that I wish I could believe and get what you have. But I've blamed Him so long for all I've suffered that it will be hard for me to believe He could love me enough to forgive me and take me in as He took you."

Elise knelt beside her and put an arm around her. "He loved you enough to die for you," she insisted. "The Bible tells me that while we were yet sinners,

Christ died for us. None of us deserve His love or His salvation, but that is what makes it so wonderful — that He gives it anyway, when we really want it and ask for it."

Madame got to her feet and said slowly, "Some day, maybe, but not now. Maybe some day you'll read to me from your Bible. I want to know more." Her voice trailed off into silence as she hobbled from the room.

Elise knelt beside her cot and prayed earnestly that soon the seed sown might bear fruit in the old lady's heart. As she took up her sewing once more there were tears in her eyes but there was a song in her heart. She was doing the thing for which the Lord had spared her. Perhaps this was the reason for her being here in this new land where no one seemed to know anything at all about the love of God.

CHAPTER 9

Winter came to the settlement, with sun-drenched days and cool nights. It was an unusually mild winter and there were frequent parties on the batture beyond the low levee. The young people met there and built large bonfires, roasted potatoes and oysters, played games and enjoyed themselves to the fullest. There were few homes large enough to entertain these groups; so whenever the weather permitted, they met on the river batture.

Elise went to a number of these affairs. Damont had persuaded her to go with him to the first one. She had gone because she felt the loneliness and monotony of her life growing upon her and she was glad of the opportunity to get away from it for a little while. She had enjoyed the first evening and looked forward to the next bonfire with eager anticipation.

She found that Damont had never attended these plebeian affairs before. His presence there was a surprise to the others, and for a while cast a damper over the gaiety. When, however, he unbent from his dignity and became one of them, they accepted him and his lovely companion and took them into their games and conversation.

On one or two occasions Damont had tried to persuade Elise to go with him to one of the periodic balls that were the highlights of the colony's social set, but she had refused.

"I don't dance," she told him.

"But you could go even if you don't," he insisted. "You would enjoy it and I'd love to teach you how to dance."

"You don't understand, Monsieur. I never have wanted to learn."

"What do you mean?" he asked in surprise.

"The Bible tells me that as a child of God I must be separated from the world." It was hard for her to speak to him of spiritual things. It had been so easy to talk to Chenier, but this man seemed so cynical, so cold, and he gave her the impression that he was never frank nor open about anything he did or said. There seemed always to be some sinister purpose behind his every act.

"What do you mean by being a child of God?" he asked with a quizzical smile.

"When one has accepted Christ as his Saviour and his sins are forgiven, he becomes a child of God. It's what Jesus called being born again."

"And you think you have been born again?" She did not like the faint mockery in his voice, but she refused to be daunted by it. He had asked for the truth and she would give it to him. He might as well know now just what she was and what she believed. She had tried before to speak to him about the Lord, but her weak attempts had been thwarted by his refusal to be drawn into anything pertaining to religion.

"I don't think it. I know it," she asserted. "And I wouldn't give that knowledge up for anything or anyone in the world."

He was silent for a moment; then, "Is that what

makes you so different from anyone I've ever met before?" he asked. This time there was no mockery in his voice nor in his eyes, but there was a desire there, desire which chilled her and brought her next words.

"Perhaps. I'm sure of one thing, however, and that is, not a single person I've met here in New Orleans seems to care about God or His love for lost men. Sometimes it makes me feel very lonely."

"If you'd only give me the chance, I could make you far less lonely," he exclaimed unguardedly.

He realized that this was an inopportune time to say this and that the words sounded inane, but they were drawn from him in spite of himself. The desire for her had become such an obsession that it transcended even his deep-seated ambition.

"Just let me say this," he continued as she raised a protecting hand, "I know I promised not to annoy you by telling you how much I love you, but I'm sure that if you'd marry me, you'd never be sorry. I know I could make you happy and I'd love you so much that you'd learn to love me. I'd even take you back to Paris, if that would make you happy." This last statement surprised himself and he knew that it was a lie, for he knew that he'd never dare go back to Paris even if he wanted to and he didn't want to as long as there was the hope of becoming governor of the colony.

She smiled a sad little smile and shook her head. "Even taking me back to Paris wouldn't make me happy if I married you, Monsieur. I could never be happy unless there was peace in my heart and there could never be peace in my heart if I married someone who wasn't a Christian."

He gave her a puzzled look. An invisible wall was standing between them, he realized, a wall that seemed to surround her. It was this strange barrier which was keeping her so unapproachable and so remote in spite of all his efforts to win her. It irritated him, yet it frightened him.

"Do you mean that you'd never marry anyone, even if you loved him, if he didn't think just as you do about this strange religion of yours?" he asked.

"This isn't any strange religion," she corrected him. "What I believe and what I think, is found in God's word and there is nothing new or strange about it. It's what you have here and what is practiced all over the world in the name of religion that is new and strange. I wouldn't try to control the thoughts of the man I should marry, but he would have to believe in the Lord Jesus Christ as his own personal Saviour."

"Suppose you should fall in love with someone who is as much a heathen as I am?" he asked. He was thinking of Chenier. Perhaps she was in love with him already and this was just an act to mislead him and keep the truth from him. He had never encountered truth nor sincerity in any woman. She must be like all the rest even if she did seem so different.

"I wouldn't let myself fall in love with him."

"Love is something that we don't seem able to control," he said, with a tinge of bitterness in his voice. "If it were, I wouldn't be so much in love with you when you've given me so little hope. It's rather humiliating," he confessed with a twisted smile.

"I'm sorry. You have been so wonderful to me that I wouldn't want to humiliate you or hurt you. But, as you say, we can't control love and I can't make myself love you. We can still be friends, though, can't we? I still need friends," she reminded him and laid a timid hand upon his arm.

He took it and pressed it to his lips. "Of course we can and we shall," he replied. "But I shall keep on hoping that one day we can be more than friends.

Perhaps some day I can believe as you do. Then at least one barrier will be removed."

"I hope you can," she replied but she felt what he knew within his own soul, that he had no desire to be any different from what he was. She realized, however, that she had no right to judge.

Andre Chenier had been away on one of his trips to the Indian villages where he bought his furs. When he came back to town he tried to monopolize Elise's company on the nights when the groups gathered on the batture or when smaller groups met in one of the homes where they popped corn or made candy. The others saw the growing rivalry between the two Andre's and joked about it, but a few of them who knew the two men more intimately realized that sooner or later this rivalry would bring on more serious results. In a day when duels were fought upon the slightest excuse, the love of a woman in a colony where women were so scarce could not be called a slight excuse.

Elise tried to be impartial in her friendship with the two men, but she knew from the beginning that she enjoyed Chenier's company far more than she did Damont's. She could respond to Chenier's light talk and could laugh at the amusing incidents he related to her. She was glad when he came to the house as he frequently did, having dinner with them or just sitting with her while she sewed. With Damont she could never feel quite free and unrestrained. This feeling of restraint was disturbing and she tried to overcome it, but it grew upon her the more Damont persisted in his attempts to win her.

Occasionally on the evenings when Chenier visited them Madame would sit with them for a while and Elise would make her feel welcome, glad to have the opportunity to make her life less lonely. Sometimes their conversation would turn upon spiritual realities.

The old lady as well as Chenier seemed genuinely interested in what Elise had to say. She never tried to force the subject of Christianity into the conversation. She felt that just a few words now and then were enough. She was glad that Chenier was interested. She didn't try to analyze the reason for being glad or to explain to herself why it was that she could speak so freely to him about spiritual truths while her lips seemed sealed when she tried to talk to Damont about the Lord. Something happened, however, which opened her eyes and brought a new problem to her.

On New Year's night there was a big reception held at Bienville's Hotel. The building was a large two-story structure, with wide steps and a broad gallery running across the entire front of the house. The parlors were furnished with brocaded satin draperies at the windows. French furniture with gilded woodwork and damask cushions was scattered about the room. Expensive tapestries hung on the walls, and deep-piled colorful rugs covered the floors.

It was the one big event of the year to which everyone looked forward and hoped for an invitation. Those who could afford the luxury of new clothes made elaborate preparations for the affair and when the throngs gathered on the night of the reception, the event was as gay and colorful as any in Paris had ever been. Silks and satins, velvets and brocades adorned the men as well as the women. Men with powdered hair or white wigs, women with rouged cheeks and painted lips went arm and arm down the long line toward the governor, bowing and curtsying as they exchanged greetings and well-wishes for the New Year.

Damont had invited Elise to go with him. She had consented, though she knew that she would have to sew into the small hours of the morning in order to make a dress suitable for the occasion. She had been hoping that Chenier would be her escort, but while he was out of town Damont had invited her. Chenier had not tried to conceal his disappointment when he found that his rival had gotten ahead of him.

Elise was lovely in her simple dress of dull blue. It was cut not too low in the neck and over this there was a bertha of lace which fell over her bare arms to the elbow. Her hair curled softly about her face and fell in a cluster over one shoulder where it was held in place by a band of black velvet.

When she stood taking a last glance at herself before the small mirror over the wash basin, she saw Madame standing behind her looking at her with an expression she had never seen on the wrinkled old face before.

"Will I do, do you think?" Elise asked playfully as she turned to face the old lady.

"You're very beautiful, my dear," Madame replied in the gentlest voice Elise had ever heard fall from her lips. "How I wish you were my daughter."

The words excited the girl's heart. She put her arms around the bent shoulders and kissed the withered cheek. "That's the sweetest thing you could ever say to me," she said. "I shall try to take a daughter's place, even though I know I never can."

There was feeling in Madame's voice as she said, "I never thought I'd ever love anyone again after my Joseph died, but — but —" and her voice was choked by tears.

Just then Damont came and Elise went to the door. Damont's eyes told her how pleased he was with her appearance.

"How lovely you look!" he exclaimed as his eyes traveled over her face, taking in each feature, then over the becoming dress.

"Thank you, Monsieur," she replied as she bowed with an exaggerated curtsy.

It was the first time Elise had ever seen Governor Bienville. He was dressed in a suit of brilliant red with a black waistcoat over which his ruffled stock fell in a white froth of filmy lace. His hair was powdered in the prevailing fashion, making his thin face look even more dark by contrast. His manner was gracious and his eyes lighted with admiration as Elise was introduced to him.

"I've heard of you, Mademoiselle," he remarked as Damont introduced her. "You came here under most unfortunate and unusual circumstances, but I hope that you have learned to like New Orleans and some of its citizens in spite of all that happened to bring you here."

"I am learning to love the place and many of its people," she replied after a deep curtsy. "I shall try to make myself a citizen worthy of my new home."

Bienville cast an amused glance at Damont and smiled as he said, "From what I have heard, at least one of the citizens is very much concerned that you should not be too generous with your affections."

She blushed as she turned to make way for others in line waiting to greet the governor. As they made their way toward the big punch bowls at the far end of the wide hallway, she saw Chenier and the look in his eyes brought added color to her cheeks and a more rapid beating of her heart. There was no mistaking the look in those hazel eyes. They were saying things which he had promised her he would not say again. Damont saw the look and noticed her heightened color and an unreasoning fury took possession of him. In that moment he felt that he could slay Chenier with his bare hands. The fear that Chenier's youth and his charm might win in this battle between them rose like an ugly monster that stalked him and refused to be driven away.

Chenier made his way to them through the crowd

and greeted her with a friendly smile. "My, but you look beautiful!" he remarked. "I thought you looked lovely enough out in the garden with smudges on your face, but tonight you're something to make an artist rave."

"We're not interested in artists' ravings, Monsieur," Damont interrupted. "Be kind enough to let us pass. We're on our way to the punch bowl."

"Of course," Chenier replied blandly. "I'm on my way there too. I'll go along with you."

Damont's face flamed a dull red and there was an angry spark in his eyes. "We don't need your company. Mademoiselle Demarest came with me."

Chenier ignored him and turned to Elise. "Does that mean that you can't even speak to your friends when you're with him?"

"Of course not," she replied. She was embarrassed and didn't know just how to cope with this situation. It reminded her of that first dreadful day at the home of the nuns. She didn't want to be the cause of a scene and yet she feared that there would be one when she saw the expression of the two faces before her. "Can't we all go and have some punch together? I'm sure you wouldn't mind, would you, Monsieur Damont?"

Damont could do nothing but agree, though his expression was not pleasant to see.

When they had been served with punch, Elise found that it was heavily supplied with rum. After one sip she put the glass down.

"Don't you like the punch?" Damont asked.

"No. It has liquor in it," she told him.

He turned to a servant and said, "Bring Mademoiselle a glass of orange juice."

What else was there, he wondered, that would be revealed by this amazing girl? Where did she get all this nonsense? He began to wonder what life would be like with her. Would it be worth all the effort it was costing him to try to win her? One look at her lovely face and one glance at Chenier's rapt adoring gaze made him grimly determined to possess her, no matter what life with her would be like. When she was finally married to him, things would be different. He could afford to humor her now.

When they had finished their drinks and had partaken of the sandwiches and small cakes and confections, they turned to mingle with the crowd milling about in the large rooms. Chenier refused to be shaken though Damont did everything but insult him. He ignored the threatening looks of his rival as well as the veiled hints to leave. He kept up a lively conversation with Elise in which Damont couldn't seem to enter. This made him more furious than ever, for there was nothing he could do about it.

It was at this reception that Elise first met Rosalie Allain who was so desperately in love with Damont and with whom, until her coming, Damont had been amusing himself.

Madame Allain took in the situation as soon as she met Elise. She knew now why Andre Damont had been neglecting her until she was frantic with anxiety and the fear that he no longer cared. Now she knew. He was in love with this unknown, penniless girl who had come over with the dregs of Paris and was holding herself so aloof from the many who would marry her. She felt that this was only a pose which this girl was assuming in order to increase desire in the hearts of men who were starved for love. She hated her from that first moment, not only because of Damont's evident interest in her, but because of a beauty which made her own too-ripe charms seem commonplace. She determined to do something to break up this budding romance and to bring Damont back to her side, but she knew that she would have to exercise caution and subtlety if she were to succeed.

When the reception was over and Elise and Damont were on their way home, Chenier bade them good-night and left them. Damont was too furious to acknowledge his slightly mocking bow and parting words. He knew that Chenier was laughing up his sleeve at him and gloating over the fact that he had spoiled the evening for him by practically monopolizing Elise.

As they paused for a moment in the darkness at the cottage doorway, Elise turned to him and said, "Monsieur Damont, I thank you for a most enjoyable evening. It was so good of you to invite me."

"It certainly couldn't have been my company that made the evening enjoyable," he retorted irritably. "You scarcely said a dozen words to me all evening."

"Was that my fault?" she asked innocently. "You wouldn't talk and Monsieur Chenier did. I had to be polite."

"Why didn't you send him about his business?"

"Why should I?" she asked in surprise. "I couldn't do that. He's a friend and it would have hurt him."

"He's more than a friend. You know that he's in love with you and he knew that I wanted you to myself tonight."

Suddenly he took her in his arms and held her so close that she could scarcely breathe. He bent down to kiss her, but she turned her face away and struggled to release herself.

"Kiss me," he begged. "Kiss me, Elise, Just once. I love you. I know I promised not to say it, but I can't keep that promise any longer."

"No! No!" she cried and pushed him from her almost violently. "You forget yourself, Monsieur, and you're taking advantage of my friendship. If you do this again, we can't even be friends, even though you have been so kind to me."

"I'm sorry," he said contritely as his arms fell to his sides and he bowed his head dejectedly. All the fire and anger seemed to have died within him. "I shouldn't have done it, but you were so beautiful tonight and I couldn't help being jealous of Chenier. Forgive me. I promise never to annoy you again. Will you believe me?"

"I shall try," she said coldly, "but if I have to be constantly on my guard with you, I shall be afraid to trust myself with you."

"You needn't be afraid," he assured her, "Just forgive me and forget this, won't you?"

"I shall try," she repeated. "Goodnight, Monsieur."

As he walked down the darkened street he communed with himself. "Why am I such a fool as to want her so much when she doesn't want me?"

CHAPTER 10

A few nights after the disturbing episode with Damont, Elise and Chenier went to a party at the home of Claire Aubert. The house was small and there were only two or three couples there. They popped corn and ate cookies and pecans while they told stories and laughed. Claire was proud of her home, tiny though it was, and crowded in between two larger houses, for it was the only home she had ever known. The tenement she and her parents had occupied in Paris was little more than a hovel. The cottage had but three rooms with walls that were white-washed and rough board floors, but it was immaculate and the bright curtains at the windows with a few scatter rugs on the floor made the place look homey and attractive.

Claire looked unusually pretty in the print dress that Elise had made for her. She appeared to be happy in her new life. Her young husband was genuinely in love with her. The sight of them together on this evening, their apparent happiness in their home life made Elise realize more forcibly than ever her own loneliness and a longing which she had not felt before assailed her for a home and someone to love and care for her.

When they left and started for the cottage, Chenier took Elise's hand and put it in the bend of his arm, guiding her over the uneven boards of the banquette as they strolled along. It was a cloudless night. The silver disk of a late rising moon peeped over the housetops and cast a pale sheen over the darkened town and rested upon the square-cut shingled roofs, turning them to white and emphasizing the dark silhouettes of the houses with their overhanging eaves. Far in the distance came the cry of the watchman calling out the hour of the night. The heavens were filled with myriads of glittering stars which were growing dimmer in the light of the rising moon.

"Isn't this a perfect night?" Elise remarked. "It seems as if you could almost reach up and touch those stars. 'When I consider the heavens the work of Thy fingers and the moon and stars which thou hast ordained, what is man that thou art mindful of him,'" she murmured softly as she stood a moment and gazed into the star-studded vault of the heavens.

Andre wasn't looking at the stars but at the upturned face, the white sweep of her slender throat, the lips half-parted in wonder and the eyes that complimented the moon. "You're a poet," he said simply.

"Those are not my words," she said. "David wrote them, but the Lord gave them to him. I suppose he was looking at those same stars. What a wonderful Lord we have! Just think, for thousands, perhaps millions of years, those same stars have been up there, twinkling away, just as they are tonight."

"You put God into everything, don't you?" he said as his rapt gaze still rested upon her face.

She smiled. "Why shouldn't I? He's in everything because He created everything. When you love Him, Andre, you can't help thinking of Him. He becomes a part of every waking thought."

She seldom called him Andre and whenever she did it stirred hope within his heart.

"Won't there ever be room in your thoughts or love in your heart for anyone else?" he asked.

They had reached the cottage and stood within the shadows in almost the same spot where Andre Damont and she had been a few nights before.

"I'm sure there will be," she replied as she withdrew her hand from his arm and stood facing him. "The love of God in one's heart doesn't exclude love for others. In fact it makes one love everybody."

"But I don't want you to love everybody," he protested seriously. "I want you to love me. Oh Elise, Elise, if you knew how much I love you!"

Suddenly he caught her in his arms and kissed her. It happened so unexpectedly that she couldn't have resisted him if she would; but as his lips touched hers, she felt no desire to resist him, but yielded herself to his embrace. For a moment she was lost in a strange new joy that swept through her in the clasp of his arms and the touch of his lips upon hers. Then she released herself.

"Why — why — did you do that?" It was a cry of anguish.

"Forgive me! I'm sorry if I've hurt you," he said. "I'm not sorry I kissed you. I can't ever be sorry for that because it's a memory I shall carry with me until I die. I love you so much and you're so unobtainable. You seem as far out of my reach as those stars up there and I know I shall never be good enough for you to love me. That's why I couldn't help kissing you. I promise never to do it again if you'll only let me continue to be your friend. Don't be angry with me."

Suddenly she burst into tears and fled into the house leaving him standing there shaken and bewildered. Finally he turned and went down the street.

The memory of her kiss was still warm upon his lips and there was a glow within his heart, even though his step was slow and his head bent in dejection.

Elise got ready for bed while tears still flowed. A great ache in her heart was struggling with a joy that threatened to engulf it. As she knelt beside her bed, she felt a sense of guilt as she tried to pray, guilt for the joy that possessed her. Words finally came, words which staggered through sobs.

Love had come so unexpectedly and so overwhelmingly that she felt powerless to battle against it, though she knew she must. She must prevent this love from growing; she knew, even in the first moment of awakening, that she couldn't uproot it from her heart. It was there to remain a part of her, for as long as she lived. But he must never know, for the battle would be more difficult if he should. She could never marry him until he became a Christian and he seemed as far from that as on the day she had first met him. He had listened to her whenever she talked about salvation, but that was all that he had ever done and she fancied that he only listened because he loved her and wanted to please her. She realized what a burden this would be for her to carry and that there would be a battle for her to fight, but she relied upon the One who had never failed her and she felt sure that He would give her strength to carry through.

The next morning at the Market Place she again saw Chenier. He was waiting for her as he had done often before. He greeted her and took her basket, accompanying her while she made her purchases.

Throughout the place voices mingled to form a pattern of noise that smothered the peace of the lovely winter morning. Far across the river could be heard the loud clang of bells as overseers on the King's plantation gave the signal to the slaves that it was time for them to start work in the fields. Even in winter there was ground to be ploughed and crops to be planted and the slaves knew no interval of rest from their weary round of labor.

"May I carry your basket home for you?" Chenier wanted to know.

"If you wish," she said with a bright smile.

"Am I forgiven for last night?" he asked as they made their way out the Esplanade toward the cottage.

"Let's just forget it, shall we?" she replied. "It's something I'd rather not talk about."

"It's something I shall never forget," he said seriously. "But I won't mention it again. I shall have to leave again tomorrow and this time it will be a long trip — probably a month or more. I shall miss you very much."

"And I shall miss you, my friend." *If he only knew how much she would miss him,* she thought.

When he was near, there was a feeling of security within her, but when he was away, as she had realized on his first absence, she felt terribly alone and unprotected. The memory of Damont and his unrelenting pursuit of her stirred within her a faint fear. She had felt it before and had tried to banish it, feeling confidence in the God she trusted. Yet it returned every time she was with him.

"Why so quiet?" Chenier asked presently. "Do I dare hope that you're grieving over my going away?"

"I'm heartbroken. I'm desolate!" she said in tones of mock despair. Then more seriosuly, "I was thinking of what has happened to me in just a few months. How little we know of what lies ahead of us. And how fortunate that we can't know."

"How true," he agreed.

He told her goodbye at the gate and left her. Early the next morning he went up the river toward the Natchez settlement to continue his trade with the Indians. Elise missed him more than she had anticipated and realized with a shock how much he had become a part of her life. His help with her garden, his presence at the Market Place carrying her basket on so many mornings, his interesting talk and attractive personality had helped fill in many a lonely hour.

Damont came to the house as often as he could find excuse and took her to the various gatherings and parties whenever she would go. She couldn't go often for her days and nights were becoming more crowded with sewing as her list of customers grew. He made himself as indispensable as he could and he was enjoying Chenier's absence. It made him feel that perhaps he was making more progress while his rival was out of the way.

Rosalie Allain cultivated Elise's friendship adroitly and persistently. She was determined that this girl should not have Damont, for she did not want to share him with anyone — at least not anyone of the white race. She alone knew of Damont's Indian wife, White Dove. She had stumbled upon his carefully guarded secret by accident. It had not caused her a single pang of jealousy to know about this secret love affair, for morals were at such low ebb in the colony that this was nothing out of the ordinary. She had kept this knowledge to herself feeling that perhaps sometime it might come in as a useful piece of information. With Elise, however, it was different. Here was a girl who had everything in her favor, youth and beauty and an aloofness which made her even more alluring.

She had had Elise do some sewing for her, though she had slaves who always did her sewing, and this gave her an opportunity to get acquainted with the girl and to keep an eye on her while she thought out some plan that would break up what she thought to be a growing love affair between her and Damont. She had mentioned Damont casually as an old friend of hers and her husband and Elise's expressions of gratitude for what he had done for her convinced her that this girl did indeed love Damont. She had had them in for dinner several times. This was anything but pleasant for Damont, for he saw through her pretense of friendliness toward Elise, but he was helpless to do anything about it. If he refused to accept Rosalie's invitations, Elise wouldn't understand and it might give Rosalie an opportunity to reveal the true situation between them, so there was nothing for him to do but sit through the meal and a part of the evening and listen to Rosalie's honeyed words, knowing full well that behind them lay a poisoned barb which she would one day try to use to make Elise turn from him. He raged inwardly as he realized that he could do nothing but wait and hope for the best. But this knowledge made him more strongly determined than ever to win what seemed just beyond his reach.

Elise was lavish in her praise of Madame Allain. If she had not been so engrossed with her own little problem she might have wondered at Damont's half-hearted response to her enthusiasm. Perhaps, also, she would have sensed what she never suspected, the deep-seated hatred of this woman who hid that hatred beneath such a suave, charming manner. Damont, knowing Rosalie as he did, wondered where that hatred would lead. He had known that this would happen if Rosalie ever suspected the truth. It was not in his plans for her to know or suspect until he was married to Elise. But he had never dreamed that Elise would be so immune to his wooing.

CHAPTER 11

Andre Chenier returned from his trip to the Natchez country with the disturbing and horrifying news of the massacre that had just taken place in that settlement. The Natchez Indians, joined by the Chickasaws, had wiped out the whole settlement of Fort Rosalie. White prisoners taken by the Indians had been tortured before being put to death and then left as a mute and horrible warning to the whites. The news set the colony in a panic. If the powerful Natchez tribe should unite with other war-like tribes to the north and west, they could wipe out every settlement along the Mississippi before sufficient forces could be gathered to withstand them. The one thing that had kept the colonists in a measure of safety was the fact that these Indian tribes were disunited. There was constant warfare between the tribes. Now that there was danger that they might unite against the whites terror spread throughout the colony. The attack upon Fort Rosalie had been made in retaliation against French tyranny. Other tribes had suffered in the same way and this one success might inflame the whole Indian nation against the whites.

A moat was hastily dug around the city and every

precaution taken to withstand any attempt to attack the city. Vessels were anchored in the river opposite New Orleans as a possible refuge for the women and children if the Indians should attack the city. Guards were placed at the four corners of the square which formed the boundary of the town and the citizens waited tensely to see what would happen.

The market was strangely quiet and there was little to be had except what was grown within the city and along the river front just below the city. No one dared to go into the woods to hunt and no Indian came into the city. The friendly Tchouchoumas, vestige of the once great river tribe of the Houmas, lived along the banks of Bayou St. Jean, but they were warned to keep away from the city. The citizens feared treachery. They knew that their friendliness could easily be turned into animosity if stirred by the warlike tribes from the north. Consequently there was no produce brought in by their hunters who had supplied New Orleans with much of its meat.

Madame Romain was in a frenzy of fear. Her cottage was so near the outskirts of the town that she knew it would be the first to be reached if the Indians should come. It was during this time of fear and tenseness that Madame was made aware of Elise's calmness and lack of fear. The girl went about her accustomed routine as if no menace hung over the city.

Madame complained to Elise at her seeming indifference to the danger. The girl's calmness irritated her because she could not reconcile it with her own fears.

"You go about as if you don't know what the danger is," she said. "If you had lived here as long as I have, you wouldn't be so ignorant of the Indians. If they should attack us, we'd be tortured in a way you never dreamed of."

"What's the use of getting all worked up about it?" Elise asked. "Worrying doesn't help any."

"How can you help but worry when you know what might happen to us? Monsieur Chenier said that those terrible Indians had burned some of the prisoners. They found their bodies tied to stakes on the levee and burned to a crisp. They might do that to us if they come here."

"I've tried to tell you before, Madame, dear," Elise said as she sat down beside the old lady, "but you wouldn't believe me. A Christian shouldn't worry, for the Lord has told us to cast our burdens upon Him and He will sustain us. He's promised to be with us in trouble and deliver us. How can I worry and be afraid when I trust Him to take care of me?"

"But if you should be burned as those others were, how about that?" asked Madame.

Elise observed the change in the old lady. Before, when she listened without grumbling as she had done in the beginning, there was a lack of real heart interest in what she heard. But now, in the face of horrible death, with the evidence of Elise's calmness and lack of fear, she had a keener interest in the source of this calm.

"If I should be tortured, it would be terrible," Elise replied. "I shudder when I think about that. But God would give me strength to endure torture and I believe He would take away the pain. He did it for thousands of martyrs who were tortured and killed for the sake of their faith in Him and I believe He would do it for me. Even if He didn't, torture couldn't last forever and death would be just the beginning of a glorious life."

"You really believe that, don't you?" There was a strange new wistfulness in the old lady's voice.

"Of course I do." Elise took the old lady's hands in hers. "It's real, dear, what I have in my heart. It's something to live by and to die by, not just something to talk about."

"I wish I had that something," Madame sighed. "I'm so afraid that I can't sleep at night."

"You can have it just the same way I got it. It's a gift that God gives to all who really want it. Would you let me tell you how you can receive it? I've told you before but I'm afraid you didn't really listen."

Madame nodded. Elise knelt beside her chair and told her once more the old, old story of God and His love and the sacrifice of His Son on the Cross and the Atonement for the sin of all mankind. As she again unfolded the plan of salvation to her, tears rolled down Madame's withered cheek, and when Elise had finished and had asked her if she wouldn't receive this precious free gift of eternal life, she was willing to pray the sinner's prayer. Light came into the hardened heart, driving out bitterness and unreasoning fear and bringing in the joy that comes to a new creation in Jesus Christ.

"I can almost be glad that this danger has threatened us," Elise said as she wiped her own moist eyes. "If this hadn't happened, you might never have been saved. Now you have nothing to fear, not even death."

Madame shook her head slowly. "I'm not so sure about that. When I think of those Indians, I'm still afraid. How do you know I won't be afraid if they should come?"

"Because God has promised in His Word that 'as thy days, so shall thy strength be.' When the time comes, if it does, you'll find strength in that moment. You don't get it ahead of time, dear; it comes to us day by day as we need it. You will believe that, won't you?"

"I'll try. But I just hope those Indians don't come."

Elise laughed as she gave the old lady a hug. "So

do I. And I pray, for the sake of those who are not ready to die, that we will be spared."

An expedition was sent against the Indians and succeeded in driving them from their stronghold. The warlike Natchez fled and Bienville was successful in punishing the Chickasaws for becoming allies of the Natchez. Once more there was a measure of peace within the city. The much-feared coalition of the tribes was thwarted, giving the colonists time to build up their forces and call for reinforcements from France. The city once more began its accustomed activity. The saw mill and rice mill and brickyard on the lower edge of the town resumed work and the Market Place became the scene of activity once more. The social life was also resumed now that fear had passed.

With the return of the Indians to the city with their produce and handwork, Andre Damont received a shock which came near upsetting all his plans to win Elise. She had been to take some sewing to one of her customers and they had met. Damont hadn't seen her for some time, for during the excitement after the massacre he had been occupied with plans for the defense of the city. It was a chance for him to prove his worth to Bienville and a possible step up the ladder of his ambition to supplant Bienville when the time came. Bienville was getting old and was sure to be relieved of his office before too long.

As they walked along they saw an Indian girl coming toward them. She was beautiful and Elise remarked about her beauty. He scarcely heard her for at the same moment he recognized the girl as his Indian wife, White Dove. He had been led to believe that she had gone with some of her tribe when they left their village and went west just before the massacre at Fort Rosalie. He had been so engrossed with his pursuit of Elise and with his business affairs that he hadn't been to the village for some time. Her sudden appearance gave him a shock which he found difficult to conceal.

She stopped in front of them, blocking their way. Her hostile eyes rested for a moment upon Elise's lovely face, then she turned to Damont and there was fire in her eyes.

"I speak with you," she said in broken French.

Damont had but one thought, to get Elise out of the way before the girl let out his secret. He knew that it would forever remove Elise from him if she learned the truth.

"Would you forgive me, Mademoiselle, if I allow you to go on alone?" he said. "This girl must be in trouble. I'll see what I can do to help her."

"Of course," she replied and, with a smile at the unsmiling girl, she went on her way. She was so preoccupied with her own thoughts that she didn't notice Damont's nervousness and she suspected nothing.

"Who is she?" demanded White Dove as soon as Elise had left them.

"A friend. What is that to you?" he was raging inwardly that he should have to account for his actions to this girl and he longed to vent his rage upon her but he dared not. The situation was too precarious not only from the standpoint of the colony but for his own sake. He realized that one word from this girl would blast all his hopes where Elise was concerned and that one word from her, if he should arouse her jealousy or anger, might set the whole Indian situation ablaze again.

"What is that to me?" she repeated with eyes blazing. "You forget I am your wife. You make many promises. You keep none. Little papoose never see father. Why not? Why you stay away so long? You promise one day you bring me here or you come and be Indian like me. You do nothing."

Damont spoke in conciliatory tones but he kept them so with difficulty. The knowledge that he had a child filled him with dismay and a new fear. Something would have to be done, but what or when or how, he had no idea. He couldn't think clearly just now. His one thought was to get her out of town before someone else discovered his secret.

"You know I couldn't come to you when things were like they've been," he told her. "There was too much trouble. It would have been dangerous for both of us if I had come to you."

"You never came for long time before trouble," she stated. "This girl, she make you forget. But I no forget that you my husband."

"You're wrong," he retorted. "This girl is nothing to me and I don't forget that you're my wife. I'll keep my promise as soon as I can, but in the meantime you'll have to be patient. I told you that when I married you."

"Yes. I believed you then. But now I don't believe you. You lie, one great big lie. I see how you look at this girl. Same way you look at me when you love me. I should know better than to trust white man. They know nothing but lies. But you are father of little Singing Water. I will not let white girl take you from me. I will kill her first."

"Then you would be killed too," he stated, struggling to keep his voice calm. "You know that. You know that you couldn't get away with murder. They'd hunt you down and hang you like they've hanged other murderers."

"What care I if they do," she stated calmly while her eyes scanned him with scorn. "If she take you, I don't want to live. After I kill her, I be glad to die."

"I wouldn't want you to die, my White Dove," he spoke soothingly with a trace of the tenderness in his voice that she had heard in the days when he was wooing her. "You're too beautiful to harbor such thoughts. I shall come to see you and my little daughter just as soon as I can slip away. Now go home before trouble comes to you. I've explained to you why I couldn't get to the village. Believe me and just go home and wait for me."

She stared at him for a long moment before she replied. There was contempt in her glance, and scorn in her voice. "I go, but I do not wait long. While I wait, keep away from that girl."

She turned and left him standing there raging and wishing that he could plunge a knife into her back. She walked with easy, graceful stride out the street toward the Rampart without ever looking back.

After a time he turned in the direction of his home. That afternoon when he went to see Elise he mentioned the Indian girl as soon as he could do so.

"I hated to have to leave you this morning," he said, "but that girl wanted me to do something about money that was owing to her. It seems that one of the women had employed her and didn't pay her before this trouble came. She knew me, for I was a frequent visitor at the lady's home and she thought I might induce her to pay her. I suppose the lady forgot it in the excitement."

He felt that the lie was a very poor one but he hoped that she wouldn't see through it. It was the most plausible one he could think of.

"I didn't mind," she told him. "I hope you can help her get her money. She's very beautiful, isn't she? The most beautiful Indian I've ever seen."

She scarcely heard his half-hearted assent to her remark. She was thinking of Chenier. He was going away again and she would be desolate without him.

CHAPTER 12

Not long after the threat of an Indian massacre, the colonists had to face a conflict with nature. Winds from the swamps blew in swarms of mosquitoes which made life miserable for both man and beast. There were always mosquitoes in the town, but they were not too numerous nor too vicious in their attacks to be unbearable. When, however, the large swamp insects invaded in groups of hundreds of thousands and clung to their victims until they were gorged with blood, the citizens were forced to fight them. They built smudge fires around the houses and prayed for winds to blow the insects back to the swamps where they belonged.

When the mosquitoes finally left in the wake of a storm that swept across the lowlands hitting the city with winds that did much damage, something more terrifying than mosquitoes followed. A deadly fever crept into the city without warning and smote its victims with swift destruction. It began with nausea and vomiting. In a short while the patient's temperature would rise and rage for a day or two, then drop suddenly, bringing heart collapse and frequently death.

Fear filled the hearts of the citizens. This enemy was even worse than Indian menace, for it was an unseen force which struck where it would; and there was no known protection from its attack. One of the two physicians in the city was one of the first victims and the other was so overworked that he did not even try to answer the many calls for his services. There was little that he could do. The usual remedies were of no avail, and he could not cope with this unknown disease. People were calling for nurses, for many of the slaves had fled the city, preferring possible capture by the Indians to the horror of this unknown death that stalked the streets and seemed destined to enter every home. Carts trundled by laden with coffined bodies which were buried without the usual religious rites. Priests and nuns alike were victims of the disease. A pall of gloom hung over the city. The church was filled with fearful souls praying earnestly for deliverance for themselves and for the lives of those in their homes who were stricken.

When the epidemic first began, Elise laid aside her sewing and went to the homes of her friends, ministering as best she could to the sick. In many homes every member of the family was laid low and those who were recovering had no one to care for them or prepare the nourishing food that they needed to bring them back to health. She began her rounds early in the morning and didn't return to the cottage until almost dark. There was little she could do for those who were dying except to try to point them to the way of eternal life, but she found this effort brought little results. Pain-racked bodies, or those tossing in delirium or lying in the still coma of death were not fit subjects for the message of salvation to which they had turned a deaf ear for so long. She could, however, cook nourishing soup and broth for those who were recovering and her unselfish ministry saved the lives of many who would otherwise have died from sheer weakness and lack of nourishment during their convalescence.

Madame objected strenuously to this program, for she was not only afraid for herself but for Elise.

"Suppose you should take the fever," she said, "None of these people would come and nurse you. Then what would become of you?"

"God would take care of me. And I have an idea you would too," she added with a smile and a pinch of Madame's cheek. "You couldn't let your adopted daughter lie there without trying to do something to help her, could you?"

"But suppose I got the fever, too? Who'd look after us? I'd be sure to die if I got it."

"Let's not suppose," Elise advised. "God will take care of us. He has promised to supply all our needs. And if you should die, remember, you have nothing to fear now," she added gently. "Death will be just going home."

Madame was silenced, but she continued to murmur as the days passed and she saw Elise getting thinner and more worn each day. She watched her anxiously as she came in each night almost too tired to eat. Gradually a new feeling became stronger in the old lady's heart. She was not thinking of herself, nor of how she was being neglected; but her love for Elise and the new love of God which she had in her heart made her anxious for the girl's health. Elise had no time to think of herself and little time to think of Madame's needs. She prepared a simple meal for each morning and left the noon meal on the stove so that Madame could eat when she wanted to, for there were too many others who needed her more than Madame did and there were so few to help. Her own heart was torn each day by the sorrows she witnessed in the various homes, a wife or husband taken, children left as orphans, parents bereaved of children. How she longed to be able to comfort them, but hearts seemed hardened and minds blinded to the blessed truth which would have brought comfort and help in this time of need.

Annette was stricken early in the epidemic, but her strong constitution withstood the attack. With the help of Elise's faithful ministry, she and her husband recovered.

"I can't ever forget what you've done for me," she told Elise when she was strong enough to take care of herself and her husband who was still convalescing. "You risked your life for me. I can't understand why."

"I didn't want to lose a good customer." Elise replied with a twinkle in her eye.

Annette was too serious to smile at the little attempt at humor. "You did it because you're the most wonderful person I've ever known," she said.

"I did it because I love you, Annette, and because of the love of Someone who laid down His life for me. I'm not wonderful at all, but He is. I wish you could believe in Him as I do."

"You almost make me believe there is a God," Annette sighed. "But I could never believe in Him the same way you do. I've hated His name and blasphemed it too often for Him to ever forgive me, if He really exists."

Elise shook her head. "You could never go beyond His love nor His forgiveness. One day you're going to own Him as your Lord. I know it, for I've prayed for you too long and I have assurance that God will answer my prayers."

It was the first time she had ever been able to say this much without having Annette cut her short with a scornful word, but now there were tears in Annette's eyes and she shook her head sadly.

"I'm afraid that'll never be. But just keep on praying. I never had anyone to pray for me before. I really knew what fear was when I thought I was dying. It's terrible, isn't it, to think that at any moment you may stop breathing? You begin to wonder if, after all, there is a hereafter and — a hell. If there is, then I guess that's where I would have gone if I had died."

"I believe that God spared you to give you another chance. Please think about that, won't you? And don't shut your heart to the pleading of the Holy Spirit if He should call you to repentance."

"I don't understand what you're talking about, but we'll talk about it again some time, shall we?" Annette replied.

Elise was wise enough not to continue the conversation longer.

Claire was stricken also, just after Annette had recovered. Her husband came for Elise early one morning.

"Claire has the fever," he told her in distress, "and she asked me to come for you. I'm afraid she's going to die."

They hastened through the darkened streets and came at last to the small cottage. There was a candle burning in the room and by its feeble light Elise could see that Claire was fighting a losing battle with the disease. She had been stricken just two days before. The fever had raged to its height and then suddenly had left, leaving her pale and weak, with sunken cheeks, and eyes darkly circled. She lay there quietly, scarcely seeming to breathe. Elise's heart contracted with sudden pain. She had learned to love Claire dearly, and though the girl had never given her another opportunity to speak a word about salvation, they were together frequently and had become close friends. She had helped Claire plan the little clothes for the baby who was soon to come to their home and they had many happy hours cutting and sewing the little garments.

Claire's husband stood helpless at the foot of the bed while Elise knelt down beside her. He had told Elise that he had gone for her the day before when Claire seemed so much worse, but he hadn't been able to find her. She didn't know that Madame had purposely kept the knowledge from her, for the old woman felt that Elise needed rest. She had wanted to save the girl from another all-night vigil.

"Claire, dear, this is Elise. Can you hear me?" She was afraid that Claire had already lapsed into a coma and wouldn't be able to hear what she was so desperately anxious to tell her.

Claire opened her eyes and looked at Elise. For a moment it seemed that she didn't recognize her, then her lips parted in a faint smile. "I'm glad you got here in time," she whispered. "I'm — dying."

Her eyes flew open and she stared at Elise with frightened gaze. "I'm afraid, Elise! Afraid to die!" Her eyes closed, but her lips moved. "The storm! I was so afraid then. I promised I'd think about God. But I kept putting it off. Now it's too late, and I'm afraid, more afraid than I've ever been before."

Elise leaned over and spoke softly. "It isn't too late, Claire. Just listen to me. God is willing to forgive you and save your soul if you'll only believe His word and trust Him for salvation. You remember once I told you that His word says, 'Whosoever shall call upon the name of the Lord shall be saved.' That means you, Claire. Just call upon Him to save you. He's promised that He will, and His word is true. He can't fail to keep His promise. Do it now, Claire, before it is too late."

Tears ran down Elise's face as she realized that each breath might be the last and that Claire might enter eternity without the Lord.

Claire opened her eyes again and looked into Elise's

face. "Why are you crying?" she asked weakly. "Is someone dying?"

Elise realized with a sinking heart that the dying girl's mind was beginning to wander. She tried desperately to bring her back to the knowledge of her own need.

"Yes, Claire, someone is dying and that someone is you. Listen to me, please! Open your heart to the Lord and ask Him to forgive you and save you. Do it now, before it's too late. Do it now, Claire."

"Are you sure it isn't too late?" The girl's voice quavered. "You told me once that I had promised and I didn't keep my promise. Can God forgive me when I did that?"

"Yes! Yes! Just believe and trust Him. He'll save you."

Bending closer, Elise quickly, desperately, told Claire of the thief on the Cross, of the publican who smote upon his breast and said, "God be merciful to me, a sinner," and tried to make her understand that the Lord Jesus was abundantly able to save her.

As she talked, she prayed that the word of God would take hold of Claire's heart and that the voice of the Holy Spirit would be heard as her soul hung in the balance in the face of eternity. Finally the dim eyes opened, and a faint smile again parted the parched lips.

"I understand," she said, her voice barely audible. "I've been such a terrible sinner, to put God off for so long. But He is merciful. Oh God, wilt Thou forgive me? I'm sorry I failed Thee. Forgive me and save me, for Jesus' sake."

"I thank Thee, Lord. I thank Thee," Elise whispered as she bowed her head.

The sound of a man's sobbing broke the silence. Claire looked at her husband standing at the foot of the bed crying aloud in the agony of his grief.

"Tony, come and kneel beside me," the weak voice called.

Obediently he came and knelt by his wife's side.

"I want you to ask the Lord to save you," she told him. "He's saved me and He can save you. If you don't do this, I'll never see you again, but if you do, we'll meet again some day, won't we, Elise?"

"Yes, Yes," Elise replied with a voice shaken with sobs.

Tony buried his face upon the bed and asked forgiveness in a voice choked with sobs. Elise knelt beside him and added her voice to his in a prayer for faith for them both. When the two arose from their knees, Claire was still and silent. Her soul had gone out to meet the God upon whom she had turned her back for so long, but who, in His long suffering, had given her eternal life. Tony turned away in a paroxysm of grief.

Two days later he was also stricken with the dread fever, and in three days his body was laid beside Claire's in the fast-growing cemetery outside the city.

Elise went about her errands of mercy with a heavy heart, for she knew that she would miss Claire. But how glad she was for Claire's confession. Perhaps, she told herself, God knew that it would take such a situation as this to win the husband to Himself.

One afternoon, a short time afterward, as she was returning home early, utterly spent and worn, she met Chenier. Having been away for some time, he was shocked at the change in her. She was pale and thin, and the lovely eyes looked out from a haggard face. She greeted him with a wan smile.

"Elise, my dearest," he exclaimed involuntarily. The endearment brought a surge of color to her face.

She had not realized in all the hours of sickness and sorrow and death how much she had missed him, and how good it was to know that he loved her.

"What's happened?" he wanted to know. "Have you had the fever?"

"No, but I'm as tired as if I had had it. I've been trying to help those who needed help badly and couldn't get anyone else to help them. There's been so much suffering here, Andre."

"Yes, I know. But you're killing yourself. You can't go on like this. If you should take the fever, you wouldn't have strength enough to fight it. Oh, Elise, if you should die, I couldn't stand it!" he cried and took both her hands in his.

She let him hold her hands, for she didn't have the strength to resist the desire in her own heart.

"I was hoping you wouldn't come back until the fever had died out," she heard herself saying.

She was scarcely conscious of what she was saying, for the look in those hazel eyes brought such a rebellious desire to her heart. She wanted more than anything else to be held in his arms and have him kiss her once more. "You might take the fever, too," she added.

"Would it matter to you if I should die?" he asked as his hold upon her hands tightened.

"What a foolish question!" she cried. "Of course it would. I couldn't bear it if you should die!"

He tried to draw her to him, but she held him off. "I mean, you're not ready to meet God, Andre."

The light that had leaped into his eyes died suddenly. She saw the look of disappointment upon his face as he said, "Oh! Is that the only reason? I was hoping that you cared for me, just a little."

She longed to tell him the truth, that she did care, more than she had ever dreamed she could care for any man; but instead she said with a playful smile, "I do care, very much, my friend." Then more seriously, "I've lost so many friends in these last few days that I shall feel terribly lonely. Most of them knew and cared so little about God. Oh Andre, if you would only become a Christian, I'd be the happiest person in the world."

"If it would make you love me, I'd try," he said as he allowed her to release her hands.

She shook her head. "It doesn't come that way, Andre. I've told you that before. Unless you have a definite consciousness of your own sin, and lost condition and accept Christ because of Him and not because of me. It wouldn't mean anything. Let's go home. I'm terribly tired."

They turned down the street toward the cottage. Just a short distance away Damont had observed the little scene, and jealousy again stirred within him. They were so absorbed in each other that they had not seen him. He followed them at a distance while one scheme after another of getting rid of Chenier revolved through his mind. Something must be done, or his whole dream would end. Either Chenier would win her, or she would find out the truth about White Dove, or Rosalie would project some plot to defeat him.

When the two reached Madame's cottage, he followed them and repeated Chenier's tactics at Bienville's reception. He entered upon Elise's invitation and took possession of the conversation. He showed his concern over Elise's overworked condition and urged her to take more rest. He rambled on at length, determined not to give Chenier an opportunity to say anything. Elise realized the situation and felt the strain, but was powerless to do anything about it. Chenier also saw what Damont was up to and suddenly he blurted out, "If you're so concerned about Mademoiselle's health, why don't you get out and give her a chance to rest? Can't you see that she's worn out? Let's both go," and he arose to his feet.

Damont sat still. Chenier turned to Elise and said, "Isn't it true that you need rest?"

"Yes, it is," she admitted. "I believe I would like to lie down for a little while. I'll have to go back to Madame Bronson's this evening."

Outside, Chenier turned to Damont and there was a spark in his eye.

"That wasn't so smart of you," he said. "You can't make a woman love you by playing the fool as you did just now."

"I was merely imitating your tactics, my friend," Damont smiled sardonically.

"You did a mighty poor imitation," Chenier retorted. "Why don't you go on back to your Rosalie and let my girl alone? She wouldn't wipe her foot on you if she knew the truth about that affair of yours."

Damont's face went white. He had no idea that anyone knew of his affair with Rosalie, least of all this rival of his.

"I shall have to challenge you one day, after all," he said slowly. "I'd hate to do that, because I know as well as you do that you'd be no match against me."

Chenier laughed harshly. "You'd be afraid to challenge me, for if you should kill me, you know she'd never look at you again."

"Is that why you're so brazen with your insults?" Damont asked. "That's what I would call hiding behind a woman's skirts."

"One more remark like that and I'll fight you here without waiting for any challenge. I may not be as skilled with a sword as you, but I have an idea that I can lay you flat in a fist fight."

"I assume you'll hold your supposed knowledge of what you call my affair as a threat over me," remarked Damont and though he tried to conceal his fear, it was evident to Chenier. "You'd love to tell

Mademoiselle about it even though there is no truth in it."

"That's a good one! No truth in it! Then why are you so afraid I'll tell Mademoiselle about it? But don't be afraid, *friend.* I have sense enough to know that a tale bearer never does himself any good. If I win her, I'll do it fairly. Just you see that you don't try any tricks. I love her enough to want her to be happy above everything else, even if she never loves me. All you want is to get her. I'll do everything in the world to win her, but I'll do it in the right way. I'm warning you to do the same."

Each man felt as they parted that, one day, in this desperate battle that they had begun, one of them must fall, perhaps fatally. And each man swore within his own heart that he would not be the one.

CHAPTER 13

The fever left as suddenly and mysteriously as it had come. Those who had lost loved ones took up the broken thread of their lives and carried on as time moved relentlessly forward. Children who had been orphaned were taken in by kind-hearted friends and adopted or kept until arrangements could be made to send them back to relatives in the homeland.

Elise's heart ached every time she passed the little home of which Claire had been so proud, for it was now so desolate and lonely. Finally a new family moved in, and it seemed a desecration to her to see others occupy the tiny cottage. It was such a comfort to know that God had spared Claire long enough for her to receive salvation. How longsuffering and merciful God was! It was so true that He was not willing that any should perish but that all should come to everlasting life. If Andre could only see and believe!

Both she and Madame had escaped the fever, and they offered up a prayer of thanksgiving that they had been spared. When the epidemic was definitely over, the social life was once more resumed. Lavish balls in the one big ball room and smaller parties in the homes took place at frequent intervals. Life seemed monotonous without these gay affairs.

One evening there was a party at one of the larger homes to which Elise had been invited. Chenier was eager to be her escort and hastened to her home as soon as he learned that he too was invited. At the gate he met Damont who was coming there for the same purpose. They had not met since their conversation several weeks before. They stopped for a moment while they eyed each other hostilely.

"I suppose you're coming to ask Mademoiselle Elise if you may escort her to the party?" Damont remarked to Chenier.

"Yes, and I suppose you're here for the same purpose," Chenier shot back in the same tone.

"You're a mind reader," replied Damont with a twisted smile. "This is as good a time as any to see which of us she prefers to go with."

Together they went to the door and waited for Elise to answer their knock.

"Does this remind you of anything?" Chenier asked as they went in.

"I'm afraid I'm stupid, but I don't believe it does," she said with a puzzled look in her eyes.

"Remember that first day at the nuns' home when we both demanded that you marry one of us?"

"Of course! I thought there'd be a fight before my eyes right there in the room."

"Well, we're both back again asking that you consider our request."

She gave them a mischievous smile. "This is so sudden, messieurs! You wouldn't want to marry me tonight, would you?"

Damont smiled and fell into her mood. "We would, if you would, Mademoiselle," and he gave her an exaggerated bow. "But which of us would it be?"

Chenier interrupted. "We want you to go to the party with one of us. We met at the gate. I was hoping I'd get here first, but I didn't quite make it. Now that we're both here, its up to you to decide which shall be your escort. I'm hoping that it will be me, of course," he ended with a grin.

"And of course I'm hoping to be the lucky one," Damont said.

She regarded them with serious eyes. She knew that whichever one she chose, the other would be hurt and angry. She couldn't let that happen.

"Both of you have been wonderful to me, such good friends, that I couldn't possibly decide between you. I suggest that you draw straws, if this is so important to you."

"That's fair enough," agreed Chenier after a moment's hesitation.

Damont was forced to agree.

She picked a straw from the broom and broke it in two. Turning her back she arranged the pieces between her fingers.

"The longer one gets the prize," she smiled.

They drew and Chenier uttered a howl of glee. "I've got the longest, so you're mine for tomorrow night at least."

Damont's keen eyes saw the sudden light in Elise's which Chenier himself failed to see, and it gave him a sick feeling of defeat. This girl was falling in love with Chenier, even though she might not realize it, he told himself. But that knowledge made him more determined than ever that Chenier should never have her. He admitted his defeat as gracefully as he could and left soon afterwards. As he walked down the street toward town, an idea was born in his brain, an idea which he was determined to carry out at the earliest opportunity.

The party was a gay affair, with games and songs and merry conversation. Elise enjoyed the evening to the fullest. It was a welcome relief from the long strain of sickness and sorrow. Damont did not appear, and she felt a sense of relief at his absence. She always felt his eyes watching her every move when the three of them were togther, and it gave her the uneasy feeling that there was something sinister behind those cold eyes which belied the smiling lips and the gracious manner.

Damont was having troubles of his own while the party was in progress. He had met Rosalie and her husband that evening, and she had insisted upon his coming to their home for dinner. She gave the invitation in such a way that he could not very well refuse. After dinner her husband, stupidly unsuspicious of the affair between them, left for a meeting. He asked Damont to remain until he returned.

"Rosalie will be lonesome," he explained, "and I'm sure you can help her to pass the time until I return. I won't be gone long."

There was nothing else for Damont to do but consent. It was what Rosalie had hoped for. As soon as her husband had left, she turned to Damont with a smile which she sought to make alluring and which would have accomplished its purpose in the past but failed to stir him now.

"You've been a very neglectful friend, lately, Andre," she chided. "You haven't been near me for ages."

"You forget that there has been an epidemic, my dear Rosalie," he replied. "I couldn't very well come visiting then. No one wanted company at a time like that."

"That had nothing to do with it," she said while the smile vanished and a hard light crept into her eyes. "You've been engrossed in your pursuit of that girl and you haven't given me a thought."

"What ever put that idea in your head?" he asked.

"My two eyes," she retorted. "I'm not as big a fool as you may think, Andre."

"You're altogether adorable," he said and gave her a look he had so often given her before. But this time there was no answering warmth in her glance. "Why should I want to pursue anyone when I have you?"

"That I would like for you to answer. Perhaps it's because you're too sure of me that you take time out to pursue some newer attraction. But you won't get away with it. I'm warning you to stop before you get too deeply involved with this girl. You'll never be able to marry her, if that's what you're trying to accomplish."

"And why shouldn't I marry her, my dear? Aren't you married? Am I to be condemned to bachelorhood while you enjoy the companionship of a husband, just because I've fallen a victim to your charms?"

"Bachelorhood!" she scoffed. She was thinking of White Dove. "You were content with it until this girl came along."

"But even if I married her, and I assure you that I'm far from accomplishing that, would that need to make any difference on our relations?"

"It would make a big difference and you know it. You're in love with her and I don't intend to share you with her."

"Don't I share you with your husband?"

"Bah! You know you don't! I loathe him! He's old and stupid and I only married him because there was no one else, and he had money. You know that. You know also that if I had known you before I married him, things would have been different. I would never have married him."

She came close and put her hands upon his shoulders. Once the touch of those slim white hands would have thrilled him, but now their touch left him cold. "You made me love you, Andre, my dearest, when I didn't want to. I was honestly trying to love my husband. But you made me loathe him when I fell in love with you. Do you think I'd let that little chit of a girl take you away from me? I'd kill her first!"

He took her hands and held them, though there was no warmth in his clasp. "If you did that, then you'd surely lose me," he reminded her. "You'd be hanged for murder and I'd lose you both." He gave her a smile.

"There would be some satisfaction even in that," she countered spitefully. "If my husband knew the truth, I fancy there would be a duel," she added as her somber eyes gazed into his.

"Then you might lose us both," he countered. He drew her to him and kissed her cold lips. "Don't worry about something that may never happen," he advised. "And don't make any threats that you may never have reason to fulfill. They make neither of us any happier."

She was silent, content for the moment to be once again within his arms. In her heart, however, there was the unyielding determination that he should never marry this girl who threatened her own desires. She knew that her husband was getting old and she was living in the hope that one day she would be free to marry Andre. She had hoped, in her evil scheming heart, that he would die during the epidemic, but they had both escaped the fever.

When Damont finally left her, mingled emotions seethed within him. Rage at his impotence to win Elise's love at once, fear that she would realize her love for Chenier before he was put out of the way, unreasoning anger toward Rosalie who had him so trapped that he would have to watch his step carefully or calamity would fall upon him while he was helpless to avert it. And always in the back of his mind the thought of White Dove remained like a small, tough animal unwilling to be killed.

CHAPTER 14

Andre Chenier had received a summons from the governor. Curiosity lent speed to his free and easy stride as he walked along the Rue St. Peter to Bienville's mansion. He had never before received a summons from Bienville.

This was the busy time of the day and the narrow streets were alive with people and noisy with the rumbling of carts laden with produce and going toward the Market Place or down to the levee to unload upon one of the boats going up the river. A cloud of black dust hung over the street, for it had not rained in some days and what had been a sea of mud had turned into a grimy powder.

Merchants were busy in the small shops dusting off counters and displaying their wares to the customers who stood about the doorways gossiping before going inside to make their purchases. Tall willows on the batture outside the low levee dipped their green plumes into the yellowed stream of the river as it swirled past on its way to the Gulf.

Chenier was ushered into the governor's office.

"Sit down, Monsieur," Bienville invited, and Chenier sat in the large arm chair facing the desk.

"You no doubt wonder why I have sent for you," Bienville began.

"Yes, I do," Chenier admitted.

"There is a mission I would like to have you perform. It is for the safety of the colony."

"Yes?" Chenier was wondering what he had in mind. It wasn't usual for a *coureur de bois* to be sent upon a mission by the governor. At least he had never heard of such a thing being done before.

"You know, of course," Bienville continued, "that after the massacre at Fort Rosalie, we feared a coalition of the Indian nations against the whites. You know also what that would mean for us. Perhaps not annihilation, but surely terrible slaughter and suffering. We have heard a rumor that the Punicas are trying to form a coalition with the defeated Natchez. The Natchez are still smarting under their recent defeat and the Punicas are trying to stir them up to make an attack on the small settlements west of Natchez. At least that is what we have rumor of. If they should succeed in this, they might try to attack us. They could persuade other tribes to join them if they were successful a second time in wiping out a settlement."

"They could, but I don't believe they have any such thing in mind," Chenier said, "I was in Punica territory not long ago and I didn't see any evidence of any such plans."

"Perhaps not. But if they had such plans, would you have noticed any preparation if you were not on the look-out for it?" Bienville asked. "Our information came from reliable sources."

"I'm sure I would have sensed it if something was afoot. I haven't been trading with these fellows all this time without being pretty familiar with their activities. Even if their plans were secret, I believe I could have sensed it. Indians are pretty keen, but so are we *coureurs de bois,"* he smiled. "May I ask the source of your information?"

"I may not give you that," the governor informed him. "It came to Monsieur Damont. That is all I can tell you."

Chenier stiffened immediately. His alert mind, trained by being in the constant presence of danger, sensed something behind this affair that he didn't like. A sixth sense warned him that if Damont were connected with this information, there was something behind it of which perhaps Bienville wasn't aware. He knew Damont for what he was, a heartless schemer. Bienville knew him only as a helpful adviser who had given good advice on previous occasions.

Bienville was speaking again. "What I want you to do is to go to these two tribes to see what you can find out. Monsieur Damont says there is no better *coureur de bois* in the colony than you and that if anyone can find out the truth, you can. When you make your report then we shall know just what steps to take. There is no need to stir the colonists up again if there is no real danger. Will you undertake the mission, Monsieur Chenier?"

Chenier's mind was busy. Just why had Damont praised him to Bienville? Why had he stirred up Bienville's fears about the Indians? He knew from his frequent contacts with them that they had no such plans. Just now they were a cowed and defeated, though sullen, people. As he had told Bienville, he would have sensed it if there had been any plans for a coalition or an attack.

"Did you hear me, Monsieur?" Bienville asked impatiently. "Will you undertake the mission or shall I look for someone else?"

"I beg your pardon, Excellency," Chenier said, "Of course I shall go if you wish me to, but I repeat that there is no need for me to go. When do you wish me to start?"

"The sooner the better. Tomorrow if you can. I shall have a small company go with you for protection. Monsieur Damont suggested this."

"Damont is a fool," Chenier exploded. "Or else he wants to bring on trouble where there is none."

"What do you mean by that?" the harsh voice of the governor demanded. His dark face flushed and in his eyes there was an angry spark.

"I mean that no one but a fool would send a scout out with a band of blundering soldiers. The Indians would know they were coming long before they got near their encampment and they'd either be roused to anger and start trouble or be frightened into starting it. And we'd find out nothing. You should realize that, Governor. If I go, I'll go alone or it will be useless for me to go. I'm wondering why Monsieur Damont is so concerned for my safety."

"Because he's your friend. He spoke of you in the highest terms. I don't like your attitude, Monsieur." The governor's voice was frigid.

"I beg your pardon if I've offended you, your Excellency," Chenier said. "And I am deeply grateful to Monsieur Damont for speaking so highly of me." Bienville missed the sarcasm in his voice. "I shall leave at dawn tomorrow." He bowed and left the governor.

As he went out upon the street his mind was busy with many questions. Why had Damont stirred up the fears of Bienville and his staff? He knew that there was no such danger existing at present, but he knew that he couldn't convince them until he had gone upon this mission. Why had Damont praised him so highly to the governor? It was no love that Damont had for him. There was but one reason that he could imagine. Damont wanted him out of the way for some reason. Well, he'd not be out of the way for long;

and if Damont's plotting had anything to do with Elise, he'd be sorry.

Little did he know just what did lay behind that plan of Damont's.

Later that same day Damont was talking to a rough looking citizen known as Pierre Laclede. Laclede was arguing with him most vehemently.

"What you're asking me to do is just plain murder."

"And when did just plain murder begin to seem terrible to you?" asked Damont with a sneer.

"What d'ya mean by that?" Laclede wanted to know.

"I mean that this wouldn't be the first time you have killed a man."

"No, I guess it wouldn't be," the fellow admitted. "Everybody knows I shot Stan Norwood, but it was in a fair fight. This is different. Killing a fellow in cold blood when I don't have anything against him is different."

"I'm not talking about the killing of Norwood. I don't believe you could kill anybody in a fair fight, because you don't know the meaning of the word. But that's beside the point. I'm talking about another killing that you think no one knows anything about."

The fear in Laclede's eyes was barely noticeable, but it was there. "What're you talkin' about?" he snarled.

"I'm talking about the thing that happened just before the massacre at Fort Rosalie. There was a body there with those others, the body of your buddy. It was partially burned. But it wasn't burned by the Indians. You killed him after the massacre and hauled his body there so that it could be found with those others."

"I don't know what you're talkin' about," Laclede cried, but his white face and fear-filled eyes belied his words.

"Yes you do. You know that you killed and robbed him, and thought you'd get away with it."

"How did you know about it?"

"You don't have to know that."

"You can't prove a thing on me," Laclede muttered, but his voice had lost its belligerence.

"Yes, I can. I have the proof in my possession or I wouldn't be making this accusation. You weren't quite clever enough, my friend. You left your blanket and the knife with which you killed him too near the scene. I have them both. I've kept them for just such a time as this. Now, either do what I've offered to pay you well for doing or face the gallows. I can bring charges against you and prove them."

"But if I kill this fellow, you'll have me for two murders. What will that get me?"

"I'll destroy the evidence of this other affair when you have done what I want done. If you have any doubts about my keeping my word, you'll have enough money to take you out of the colony."

"Why are you so anxious to get rid of this man?" Laclede asked while his small beady eyes glared at Damont.

"That's my business. All you have to know is that I want it done. Now do you take the job and get the money or do I have to turn you in for murdering Norwood?"

"If you did, I'd tell them what you wanted me to do," Laclede threatened.

Damont laughed disdainfully. "Who would believe you? Now do we strike a bargain or not? Make up your mind."

"When do I leave?" Laclede asked surlily, acknowledging defeat.

"He leaves at dawn tomorrow. Keep a watch on his house and follow him. You know the trail well enough to keep at a good distance so that he won't suspect that he's being followed. When he makes camp, be ready to strike. Don't fail."

"You're not a man. You're a devil," Laclede said and spat on the floor as he turned to leave.

Damont's pale face flushed and his eyes flashed at the insult, but he was forced to take it in silence.

CHAPTER 15

The morning was damp and foggy as Chenier left his house and started on his journey. Mist hung over the trail that led through the swamps. Birds chirped in subdued tones as they waited for the mist to clear with the rising sun. Chenier cut through the swamps and headed north toward the farthest Punica settlement. His thoughts still wrestled with the questions he had mulled over since his talk with Bienville. He knew that there was some trap set for him, or he would not have been sent upon this useless mission. He knew that Damont's suggestion of a bodyguard was just a ruse, for Damont would know that he would refuse such a silly suggestion. Why Damont had done this, he couldn't imagine, unless it was to cover up some scheme of his. He was sure of one thing: whatever scheme Damont had in mind, it was prompted by his desire for Elise. In spite of his warning, Damont wasn't playing fair. Some trap was being set for him and he'd have to be on guard. Murder had not entered his suspicions. He didn't dream that Damont would go that far.

As the day advanced and he plodded on, his mind and eyes alert for any sight or sound that might warn him of what he had been sent to discover, he had the feeling that he was being followed. It was that sixth sense which an alert woodsman somehow develops on his frequent forest journeys, a warning of danger when danger is not visible. Many times it had saved him from being bitten by a poisonous snake lying concealed in the undergrowth, and often it had warned him of the stealthy approach of some inquisitive Indian who had mistaken him for an enemy.

This feeling grew stronger as night approached. He had already used his woodsman's strategy of stepping behind a clump of thick undergrowth and reversing his steps, hoping to come upon the person or animal trailing him, but he saw no one. When darkness came, he stopped in a small clearing and made his camp for the night. The night was warm and there would be no need for his blanket for covering, but he rolled it and laid it where he would sleep, leaving half of it as a shield from the fire which he would keep burning to frighten away any prowling animal. He ate his supper and sat for a while, watching the trail over which he had come, then turned in for the night. He did not go to sleep, however. That feeling of being watched kept him awake and alert. Through half closed lids he kept watch upon the bushes which almost obliterated the trail. He wondered how long he could keep up this vigil without falling to sleep, for he had come a long way that day and he was very tired. He longed for the relaxation that sleep would give. If this person, if person it was, who was following him were an Indian, he was safe, that is, if the Indian belonged to one of the tribes he had been sent to visit. If however, this fellow belonged to some strange tribe who had wandered far afield upon a mission of his own, he might fall a victim to a scalping knife or an arrow. If it were an animal he would still be in danger, for wild cats sometimes followed their prey and stalked them like their larger brothers, the leopards.

Time passed and the strain grew upon him and he felt himself getting drowsy. He dared not stir, for the thing, whatever it was, seemed to be just beyond the edge of the firelight, in the thick undergrowth. Then he heard a faint sound, just the cracking of a small branch. This told him much. It was no Indian or that branch would never have cracked. And it was no animal, or the thing would have been been ready to spring when that branch cracked. It was a man who was not too skilled in woodcraft. Just then he saw a faint point of light. It was the dying firelight gleaming upon the point of a rifle.

Acting upon impulse rather than thought, he jerked the blanket over his body and at the same time rolled rapidly out of the firelight. It was done so swiftly that the gun aimed at his body wavered an instant before it was fired. That one swift movement had saved his life, for the bullet aimed at a vital part of his body grazed his temple leaving a red streak from which the blood began to ooze.

There was a loud crashing in the undergrowth as Chenier jumped from the folds of his blanket and raced after his would-be assassin. The assassin's trail was easy to follow from the noise he made in his mad flight. In his terror and haste, the fellow stumbled over the root of a tree and fell sprawling, his gun flying from his hands. He regained his footing and turned just as Chenier came upon him. Chenier went for him with fists flying. The murderer fought back with a viciousness born of desperation. There in the darkness, without a word, they fought savagely with their fists. They were evenly matched and the outcome might have been different, but the fellow, unaccustomed to the uneven ground, stumbled again and went down under a blow from Chenier's fists. As he fell his head struck the gnarled root of a tree. There was a loud cracking sound as his skull was fractured by the impact. Chenier knelt beside him and felt for his heart beat, for he realized what that cracking sound meant. The man was dead. He hauled the limp body into the firelight and gazed down into the swarthy face of the dead man.

"Laclede!" he exclaimed. "So it was murder that my friend had planned for me. I didn't put him quite low enough."

Hauling Laclede's body back into the brush, he sat by the fire until daylight. He knew that before long that body would be preyed upon by some animal and there was nothing he could do about it. What had happened gave him no compunction. He had fought in the defense of his own life, and this fellow deserved to die. It was the law of the day. The survival of the strongest was the popular code.

The next morning he was on his way to the Punica settlement. He could go now without fear of being followed. It was as he had told Bienville. There were no signs that either the Punicas or the Natchez tribes had any plans for attack. He did some bargaining with them and left for New Orleans. On the way back he picked up Laclede's gun which he had cached along the trail. When he arrived in the city he made his way to the governor's office.

Damont had had some uneasy hours since his talk with Laclede. He had known before he sent the man upon this mission that if he succeeded, Laclede would have this dangerous knowledge to use to his own advantage. He knew Laclede well enough to know that the fellow would use it as a means of blackmail if he could. There would, of course, be the part he had played in the affair and the knowledge of Damont's evidence of that other murder to hold him off for a time, but even that would not deter him from being a constant menace. He would have to get rid of Laclede. He must think up some plan before the fellow would become annoying. He was learning the bitter lesson that one crime is but the stepping stone to another.

On this afternoon as he went to Bienville's office, he was waiting impatiently for Laclede's return. The man should have been back long before now, and he was getting more uneasy as time passed. Bienville had sent for him to discuss some other matters about the colony. He had made himself quite useful to Bienville many times and the governor sought him out frequently for his advice. The other members of Bienville's council were forced to admit that Damont's keen mind had given them good advice more than once.

It was while Damont and the governor were talking quietly that the door opened and Chenier entered. He was dressed in his woodsman's outfit of buckskin breeches and coon skin cap, and his face was covered by several days growth of beard. His eyes sought Damont's face, and there was a gleam of fire in them as he saw the sudden start and the ill-concealed alarm which showed there.

"Don't lose your breath entirely before I knock it out of you," Chenier said as he advanced toward Damont. "Get up on your feet and fight like a man, or I'll break every bone in your body while you sit there!"

Damont sat, white and speechless, eyeing him with fear-filled eyes.

Bienville clapped loudly upon his desk. "Monsieur! You forget yourself!" he cried. "What do you mean by bursting in here like this? Behave yourself if you don't want me to call the guards and have you arrested. How did you get past the guards carrying a gun?"

"Go and ask your guards what I told them. I told

them the truth. This gun isn't loaded and I'm returning it to Damont. It belongs to him."

He threw it on the floor at Damont's feet, so near that he had to jump to avoid being hit by the weapon. It fell to the floor with a loud clatter and the accompanying laughter of Chenier.

"You didn't expect it to be returned to you in this fashion, did you, *my good friend?"* he mocked.

Again Bienville clapped his hand upon his desk. His face was red and his dark eyes blazed. "I demand an explanation for this!" he cried. "You forget yourself, Monsieur Chenier! You're in the presence of the ruler of this colony."

"I'm not forgetting that, Governor. Neither am I forgetting that I'm in the presence of the biggest scoundrel that ever escaped the hangman's rope. This fellow here, who gives you such good advice and rouses your fears about possible Indian attack, sent me out upon a useless mission in order to have me murdered. That gun belongs to him. He gave it to his tool, a fellow by the name of Laclede who was to murder me on the trail. You'll find what's left of his body on the Punica trail."

Bienville turned questioning eyes upon Damont. Damont had regained his composure somewhat and faced the questioning eyes of the governor with outspread hands and a shrug of his shoulders.

"Surely you don't believe the ravings of this fellow, your Excellency," he remarked.

"I thought he was your friend," Bienville said slowly while his probing eyes remained upon Damont's still white face.

"I thought he was. I was his friend," Damont lied glibly. "I can't understand why he should trump up a thing like this. He probably killed Laclede for some reason and is trying to pin the murder on me."

"That's a lie and you know it," Chenier interjected.

"Why should I want to kill Laclede? I scarcely know the fellow. And what would make me think of trying to pin a murder on you if I didn't have the evidence right here with me? You know we're not friends. We never have been. I know you for what you are. You've always hated me because I saw through your hypocrisy. Now that we're both in love with the same girl, you want me out of the way. This conspiracy of yours to send me to the Indians was a good chance to get rid of me and blame it on the Indians. But it didn't work and now you're going to pay."

"Don't bring Mademoiselle Demarest's name into this," Damont said as he tried to regain command of himself. "Insult me if you must, but leave her name out of it."

Chenier laughed again. "I never mentioned anyone's name. You brought it in yourself. Get up and come outside and fight, if you've got any fight in you. We're going to settle this thing now, once and for all."

Bienville touched a bell and two guards appeared at the door.

"Arrest this fellow," he said.

"Just a minute, Governor," Chenier said as he stepped nearer Bienville's desk. "You claim justice for the colony; so do I. I've made a charge against this man. I demand justice for myself in the name of the King of France. You have no cause to arrest me."

"I ask that you arrest him, Excellency," Damont interrupted. "for the murder of Laclede. He shot the fellow and is trying to lay the blame upon me because of his insane jealousy."

"If you can find what's left of Laclede's body, you'll find that he wasn't shot. I knocked him down in a fair fight and his skull was cracked against the root of a tree. If you can find that skull, you'll know I'm telling the truth. The only shot fired from that gun was fired at me. Here's the mark," said Chenier pushing back his hair and revealing the red streak.

"What have you to say, Monsieur Damont?" asked Bienville. "Is this gun yours?"

"Of course not," Damont replied with just the proper shade of indignation. "I don't know to whom the gun belongs. There are no marks on it to prove that it is mine, as he claims."

"No, there are no marks upon it," Chenier admitted. "But I've seen it in your hands and you know it. Laclede could never have owned one as good as this."

"Your Excellency, perhaps Laclede is not dead at all, but has just left the colony," Damont suggested. "Suppose we let the matter rest until we can send a searching party to look for his remains." He was struggling desperately to think of a way out of this situation. "In the meantime, I'm willing to overlook the insult of Chenier's. Let him go until we have proof that Laclede is dead."

"I suppose you'd be willing to overlook the whole affair and have the governor overlook it too," Chenier cried. "But I'm not overlooking it and I'm not forgetting it. If you're not an utter coward, you'll answer my insult by fighting me fairly and not by hiring someone to murder me."

There was silence in the room. The two guards stood immobile, holding their cumbersome guns.

Bienville turned to Damont. "He has challenged you, Monsieur Damont. What do you say?" A faint seed of doubt had been sown in Bienville's mind. Chenier's anger was too genuine and Damont's coolness too forced to be real.

"Am I to be forced to fight someone with whom I have no quarrel, a man under arrest by your own orders?" Damont retorted.

His usual cool calculating mind was suddenly befogged. He felt the jaws of his own trap closing about him.

"No one is forcing you to fight, Monsieur," the governor replied calmly. "This is merely a question of defending your own honor which has been questioned. And Chenier is not under arrest. You yourself suggested his release."

Damont knew that he had been trapped. He must either fight Chenier or have himself branded a coward or worse, a suspected plotter of murder. He saw all his plans of power suddenly hanging in the balance. He saw suspicion dawning in Bienville's eyes.

He turned to Chenier and said with as much dignity as he could muster, "I shall accept your challenge, Monsieur, even though it's ridiculous to accuse me of this dastardly action. My second will wait upon you this evening."

"I don't want any duel," Chenier exploded. "What I want is to fight with my two fists, man to man."

"You've challenged me, and we'll fight with the weapons I choose," Damont informed him. "And it will be swords."

Bienville spoke to the guards and they withdrew. "You are free to go now, Monsieur. Suppose, however, you make your report, which you seem to have forgotten. Or didn't you go to the Indian settlements?"

"Yes, I went. I told you I would and I did. There were no signs of trouble. I knew there wouldn't be, before I ever went there."

He bowed to the Governor and strode from the room.

CHAPTER 16

Andre Chenier walked slowly down the street. After the heat of his anger had subsided, he could think clearly. On the return trail his mind had been obsessed with the desire to find Damont and make him pay for what he had tried to do. Now that the encounter had been made and the prospect of the duel faced him, he began to think of what he had brought upon himself. The desire to settle the affair with his fists had seemed the logical and right thing, but the thought of facing his opponent with cold steel was another matter entirely. And he well knew that he was no match for Damont. Damont was known as a master of fencing and for this reason no one had had the temerity to run the risk of being thrust through at the point of his sword.

It was not the thought of Damont's skill which caused him the most concern now, however. It was the thought of Elise and what would happen after this duel was over. One of them would perhaps be dead or seriously wounded. If he should kill Damont, which there was small chance of his doing, how would Elise feel toward him? He knew what her ideas were about so many things and he felt that if he should come to her with Damont's blood on his hands, she would turn from him and he would lose whatever hopes he might have had of winning her. He had never been so sure of his ultimate success as Damont had been, for he knew that she would never marry him unless he believed as she did about God. He had honestly tried, for her sake, to believe as she did; but somehow that belief would not come. It seemed so right for her to be as she was and to think about God and Jesus Christ as she did, but for a man like himself, it seemed too childish, too simple. He couldn't humble himself in childlike faith as she had told him he must do. But there was always the hope that someday he would be able. Once or twice he had fancied he had seen a change in her toward him, a change which gave him hope that he would win her love; but every time that hope glimmered before him, she had snuffed it out with some trivial remark or some gesture which told him that he was only imagining what he hoped for.

If he were injured or maimed for life, as frequently happened after an encounter with swords, he would be out of her life just as definitely as if he were killed. For the first time, the thought of death brought a chill of fear through him. He had faced death with reckless abandon many times in his life, but now the thought of facing a ruthless enemy who sought his life in the quiet of an early morning encounter, with none of the circumstances which had made him disregard danger in the past, brought to him a sober realization that he did not want to face it. If he had only waited until Damont was outside, where he could force him to defend himself with his bare hands, where the fire of conflict would be burned out in a fist fight, it would have been so much better. He would have satisfied the desire to fight, his anger would have died down and no one would have been too much the worse as a result.

There could be but one end to this duel, he thought ruefully. He was no swordsman and Damont would make quick work of him. For the first time in his reckless life, he began to think of what might be on the other side of this life. Was it true, what Elise had tried to tell him, that he would either go to heaven or to hell, depending upon what he did about accepting or rejecting Christ as Saviour and Lord? Until now he had brushed the thought aside when it sometimes persisted in coming to his mind. He had refused to think of anything beyond the present, even after he had been with her and heard her speak of the Christian religion. Now that this imminence of death faced him, he had to face the question of life after death. He wished, in this time of sober thought, that he had Elise's uplifting faith. She was so sure that there was life after death and that she was going to a place where all was joy unspeakable and full of glory. It would be wonderful if he could have that knowledge and could rest in it securely while that duel was being fought.

A sudden wry smile twisted his lips. If he were like she was, if he believed as she believed, he would never have gotten into a situation like this. He wouldn't be fighting any duel at all. She had taught him that much. But there was no use mulling over this now. He had a duel facing him tomorrow so that was that; and he could do nothing about it but be ready for it and do his best to put Damont out of the fight, even though he knew that to be a vain hope. With a shrug he turned in at his house and began to clean himself up.

That evening Henri Boudreaux came to see him. Damont had chosen him as one of his seconds and as the man to give Chenier due notice of the time and place of the duel. It was to be fought the next morning at sunrise on the bank of Bayou St. Jean, about half a mile beyond the home of Boudreaux. On this road which led to the lake, there was a clump of oaks and the secluded ground beneath was often used as a duelling ground.

"I don't know why he picked me for this job and I don't like it," Boudreaux said. "But Monsieur Damont has been most kind to me, and his Company has given me much work, so there wasn't anything I could do about it but agree to act for him."

"He probably didn't want his other friends to know what kind of a scoundrel he is," Chenier replied. "Don't worry about that. Just tell him that I'll be there and that I hope he gets what he deserves."

Boudreaux hastened home and broke the news to Annette. He was as much mystified as to the cause of the duel as she was, but they concluded that Elise was the real cause of the fight. They had known that sooner or later something like this would happen.

As soon as Chenier had cleaned up and had eaten, he went to see Elise. He knew that it might be the last time he would ever see her and he wanted the memory of this hour to carry with him on the tomorrow which might be his last. She had never looked lovelier to him as she stood upon the rickety front porch. She was dressed in a printed white muslin, made simply, with tight-fitting bodice and full flounced skirt. Her hair was caught up high upon her head, falling in a cluster of curls about her flushed piquant face. She had come out to get a breath of fresh air, for it was warm in the house and Madame was nodding in her chair. The night was bright. The pale glow of a full moon mantled the little garden, changing the colors of the flowers as by a magic chemistry. She was thinking of Andre as he approached with his jaunty stride and stopped at the gate. She had missed him so much.

"Greetings," he called as he came toward her.

"Don't move," he admonished as she waved a greeting to him. "Give me time to convince myself that it's really you and not some moonbeam goddess who'll vanish when I get nearer."

"My! But you're getting poetical," she replied with a smile, as he approached and stood looking at her with a light in his eyes that she had come to expect and to long to see. "Where have you been, to learn such flowery language?"

"Let's not talk about where I've been," he said as the smile left his lips while his eyes became serious. "Let's talk about you. Did you miss me while I was away?"

He sat down upon the low step and she sat beside him.

"Of course. How could I help but miss you? When you're here, you're always under foot," she added playfully.

"Is that the only reason?" he persisted, taking hold of her hand and leaning nearer so that he could see her face as she answered.

She withdrew her hand as she said. "No, not altogether. I have missed the many pleasant hours we have spent together. You have made life much less lonely for me. I've told you that before, so why should I repeat it?"

"I was hoping that there might be another reason. But why should I hope? What good would it do me if that hope was realized?"

There was a disconsolate note in his voice that she had not heard before.

"Why do you say that? Something's wrong, Andre. Tell me what it is." An unaccountable fear took possession of her.

"There's nothing particularly wrong," he said assuming his old debonair manner. "It's just that I may be going away again and I had hoped that I could carry with me the thought that you might care for me, if only a little bit."

"If you only had the Lord within your heart, you'd have everything that any girl could desire," she said, her soft tones betraying the depth of her feeling.

"Do you mean that that's all that's keeping you from loving me?" he cried as he moved nearer.

She longed to tell him that that was what she did mean, that she already loved him and was only waiting for that one thing to come to him. Instead she replied, somewhat primly, "I meant that you have so many good qualities that that one thing would make you such a wonderful person. You said you were going away again. When are you going and how long will you be gone?"

"I don't know exactly," he evaded. "I'll probably know tomorrow whether I go or stay and for how long I'll be gone. That's why I came here tonight and why I was so anxious for some word of hope to carry with me. It might help on the long journey."

"I wish I could give you that hope, Andre," she said gently, "but I can't. I shall miss you so much, my dear, dear, friend. You know that I depend upon you more than upon anyone else on earth."

"More than you do on Damont?" he asked.

"Let's not talk about him," she suggested. "He's been wonderful to me, but you and he are as different as — as night and day."

"Which am I, night or day?" he questioned, again searching for her true feelings.

"Can't you guess?" and her smile answered his.

He took her hands again and held them. "Oh, Elise, if you only realized how much I love you! Love for you has been the one good thing that has come into my life. If you never see me again, believe me, won't you, that loving you has been the most wonderful experience that has ever come to me."

She caught her breath sharply. If she never saw him again! What would life be without him? An endless stretch of sorrow and longing — and regret.

"If you never see me again," she said, trying to keep her voice steady, "remember that my last words to you were to confess your sins and to pray God to receive you as His son through the Lord, Jesus Christ. That experience would transcend anything you've ever experienced before. And it's something that even eternity could not take away from you. Oh, Andre, if you'd only believe that! I would be happy, then, even though I never saw you again in this life."

He was silent for a moment while he still held her hands. Then he released them as he said, "I've been thinking a lot about that lately. Surely there must be a life after death. I wish that I had your faith and your assurance as to where we'll be when this life of ours ends."

"You can have it, Andre, if you'll only believe what I've already told you."

"I'm afraid it may be too late for that," he said unguardedly.

"Why do you say that?" she asked in alarm.

He shrugged, realizing that he had made a slip. "When a fellow lives the life I live, he never knows what a day may bring forth."

"There's danger in this trip you're expecting to take," she said with a tremor of fear in her voice.

"There's always danger in every trip I take. Let's not talk about it any more. Let's talk about you."

"There's nothing to talk about. I can't think of anything but this trip you may take, and that I may never see you again. I should miss you very much, Andre."

He noticed the anxiety in her voice. The desire to take her once more in his arms almost overmastered him. But he did not dare to yield to that desire. She had created something new within him, a respect for womanhood which he had never known before, and the will to master his own impulses. If he should come back alive from that duel he wanted their friendship to continue. If he yielded to his desire tonight, that might remove her farther from him.

He rose and said, "I'd better be going. I have to be up before daybreak tomorrow and it's getting late." He'd better go, he told himself, while he was still master over his love and longing.

She followed him to the gate and they stood for a few moments there in the moonlight as a silence hung between them; then he took her hands and said, his voice husky with his great love, "Goodbye, Elise, my dearest."

"Goodbye, Andre," she answered in the same low tones, "and God bless and keep you."

He bent and kissed her hands, then released them and went swiftly down the street without a backward glance. As he passed a corner he met Annette going toward Elise's. He was so engrossed with his own confused thoughts that it did not occur to him to wonder why Annette should be visiting Elise at this hour.

CHAPTER 17

Annette was much upset when her husband told her of the impending duel. She knew that it would mean tragedy for Elise, no matter what the outcome might be. She was anxious to tell Elise about it, hoping that she might think of some way to prevent it but her husband had warned her not to tell anyone what he had told her. She had made up her mind that she would see Elise if she had to wait until her husband was asleep and then slip out of the house. After their evening meal he went to see someone about a job that he was to begin the next day and it gave her the opportunity she was longing for.

She was frightened when she met Chenier, for she was afraid he would guess what her mission was; but he didn't seem to notice anything unusual in meeting her. She arrived at the cottage just as Elise was going inside.

"Wait a minute," she called. "I've got something to tell you. Let's stay out here. I don't want anyone to hear what I have to say."

"Sit down," Elise invited and they sat upon the step. "What's the trouble?" she asked.

"Plenty," Annette replied. "There's going to be a duel tomorrow at daybreak between Monsieur Damont and Monsieur Chenier. Henri is to be Damont's second and he told me about it when he came home this evening. He'd be furious if he knew I had told you, but I had to let you know."

Elise uttered a startled exclamation; then sat silent for a while.

"That's what he meant when he said he might be going on a long journey," she said finally. "Oh, Annette, why are they fighting?"

"I don't know. Henri said he thought it had something to do with you."

"Why should they fight over me? I've given them no cause for that. I've tried to be friends to them both and I've tried to keep down any trouble. What weapons are they going to use?"

"Swords."

"That's better than pistols. But it's terrible! Terrible, Annette! We've got to stop them. They can't do this. They mustn't!"

"That's not the way they look at it. They call it a point of honor, the fools! To stand there and carve one another up just because of some fancied insult. But it's done so often no one thinks too much about it. I've seen duelists go by the house many times during these past months, to the oaks by the bayou, and more than once they've come back bringing a dead body with them."

"We can't let this happen. We just can't!" Elise cried, gradually beginning to realize what it might mean to Chenier — and to her.

"I thought that perhaps you could think of some way to stop this silly business. That's why I came as soon as I could get away."

"What can we do? I can't think of a thing," Elise said helplessly.

"Neither can I, I thought you might be able to think up something. I never heard of one of these fights being stopped, once it was all arranged for, but maybe you can think of something."

"Where did you say they were going to fight?"

"Under those big oaks just about half a mile from my house, on the bank of the bayou. That's where nearly all the duels are fought."

"I don't suppose it would do any good for me to go to Monsieur Damont and beg him to stop this thing," Elise suggested.

"No. You'd better go to Monsieur Chenier. He was the one who challenged Damont. Damont, as the challenged party can't do anything. If he refused to fight, he'd be branded a coward and you know he wouldn't want that to happen, not even for you."

"It would do no good to go to Monsieur Chenier," Elise said.

"Why do you think that? I thought he was so much in love with you that he'd do anything for you. I was hoping that maybe you could go to him and beg him to stop the fight."

"He'd refuse for the same reason Monsieur Damont would. Men consider their honor above anything else," Elise added with bitter emphasis.

"Yes, even if they break a woman's heart in upholding that honor. And what is honor anyway but their ideas of their own importance?"

"I must think of some way to stop it," Elise said. "I'll have to pray about it. Thank you for telling me, Annette. It was kind of you to come."

"I knew you'd want to know. I must be going, though, for Henri will be coming home soon."

They rose and Annette put her arm around Elise's shoulders. "Don't worry too much about it, dear," she advised. "After all, neither one of them may be hurt seriously. Sometimes they stop those affairs at the first drop of blood. They don't always try to kill each other."

"They will, this time, though," Elise said sadly. She knew the two men and she remembered those cold sinister eyes of Damont, his relentless pursuit of her and that feeling she had always had when in his presence. Perhaps this was the answer. He must have done something to arouse Andre to the point of challenging him. Perhaps this was what he had intended to do all along.

Annette kissed her and left her after saying, "We'll hope for the best and you just pray to your God. Perhaps He'll show you what you want to know."

Elise stood for a while at the gate, looking after Annette's retreating figure. It was the first time Annette had ever acknowledged that she believed in a God who would hear and answer prayer, but Elise was too distraught to be glad for that slight admission. Her mind was in a turmoil. A great fear consumed her, the fear that tomorrow Andre might be killed. He realized the danger; that was why he had talked as he had this evening. He knew it might be the last time he would see her. And if he died tomorrow, she'd probably never see him again for he'd be going out into eternity a lost soul. Tears ran down her cheeks and she stumbled blindly into the house and to her room where she fell to her knees and remained there in an agony of prayer.

How long she prayed, she had no idea, but exhaustion finally overcame her and, still upon her knees, she fell asleep. When she wakened, there was a faint glimmer of light in the sky, heralding the approaching dawn. Her thoughts whirled in a panic of terror. In just a little while the two men would be taking their places with drawn rapiers, ready to plunge into the encounter which might bring death to one and serious injury to the other. Without taking time to think of what she was doing, she slipped from the home and sped through the gate and up the street to the path that led along the bayou. It was a mile or more to the oaks and dawn was fast approaching. With a wordless prayer in her heart, she walked as fast as she could in the dim light, hoping that she would reach the spot before it was too late.

There was no sign of anyone stirring. The moss-draped branches of the trees overhanging the bayou made dark blotches upon the murky waters of the sluggish, winding stream. The birds began their first faint twittering as they stretched their wings and prepared to set out upon their search for food. At any other time she would have stopped to listen to their song, recognizing the melodious trilling of the mocking birds, the raucous cawing of the blue jays, with the tap-tap-tapping of the red-headed woodpecker as an accompaniment to the morning chorus. But now her whole thought was upon Andre Chenier and the danger which hung over him. She had no thought for Damont. Her love, which she had tried so long to repress, consumed her and it was agony to realize that she might never know the joy of his presence again. She was sorry now that she hadn't told him the truth last night. He could at least have had that knowledge to take with him if this were to be his last morning on earth. She heard herself speaking aloud in her agony as she almost ran along the road that paralleled the bayou. "Lord, don't let him die! I couldn't stand it! I couldn't! Please, please don't let me be too late!"

At last she approached the duelling ground. It was a small clearing beneath two huge oaks whose branches intertwined so thickly that no grass could grow underneath. It was an ideal spot for these encounters. On each side of the roadway the undergrowth was thick. She stopped in one of these clumps, a short distance from the oaks.

Dawn had come and the group had already gathered there. Chenier with his two seconds, Damont with his two, and two others, one to act as aid in bandaging up whatever wounds might be inflicted and the other to act as referee. Damont and Chenier had already taken their positions and were standing, weapons in hand, waiting for the signal to begin the duel. Damont's face was an expressionless mask and his eyes were cool and calculating. He knew his skill and he was determined to use it to make an end of his opponent as quickly as possible. Chenier's face was white and his lips were pressed firmly together while his eyes watched Damont intently. He knew that he would fight a losing battle, but he was determined to sell his life as dearly as possible. If he must die, he hoped that his enemy would go with him.

The thought of Elise came to him, making him forget for one brief moment, the deadly encounter ahead of him. How lovely she was last night! For one fleeting moment she had almost made him believe that she cared. But now it would never matter.

The call of the referee cut into his thoughts. "On guard, Messieurs!"

They raised their rapier points while each took a step forward and raised his left hand. Just then, as if she had been summoned by Chenier's thoughts of her, Elise, with ruffled skirts flying and hair falling in disorder about her face, rushed in between them crying,

"Stop! Stop! You can't do this! You must not go on with this duel."

Consternation froze the group into immobility for a moment; then Chenier uttered a cry. "Elise!" He dropped his sword arm and stared at her in amazement.

"Mademoiselle Demarest, what brought you here?" Damont asked when he found speech.

"I've come here to stop this fight. It mustn't go on!"

"Who told you about it?" Damont asked with a suspicious glance at Chenier.

"What does it matter who told me?" she retorted. "All that matters is that I got here in time. It wasn't Monsieur Chenier, if that's what you're thinking." She had seen his glance at Chenier.

The referee came to her and tried to take her hand and lead her out of the way. "Mademoiselle, this is a matter of honor. Everything has been arranged and it must be concluded. Please step aside and let us get on with this."

She jerked her hand away and faced him boldly. "I shall not step aside and I'm not going to let this go on. An affair of honor, indeed! It will be murder if one of them is killed. You know that as well as I do." She turned back to the two men, still standing between them. Her eyes watched them alertly. "I appeal to both of you to stop this fight."

There was a silence as both men stared at her. She turned to Damont. "Monsieur, you have been such a wonderful friend to me since I came here. Won't you call this affair off?"

"Mademoiselle, what you are asking is impossible, though I regret it more than I can tell you, I assure you. I've been challenged and if I refuse to fight, I shall be branded a coward and I'd be held in contempt by the lowest person in this colony."

"Wouldn't it be cowardly for you to fight with a man whom you know is no swordsman? I've been told that Monsieur Chenier doesn't know much about handling a sword and that you are one of the most expert swordsmen in the colony. It seems to me that you would be braver to call it off than to murder him in cold blood. It takes more courage to resist fighting sometimes than it does to fight."

"You're making it very hard for me to go on, Mademoiselle," he said with a note of regret, "but as the challenged party, I can't refuse to fight. Unless he should call it off, we must go on with it."

She turned to Chenier. "How about it? Will you call it off?" Her eyes were tear-filled and her voice was low and pleading.

"I can't do it. And he knows I can't." Chenier's voice was harsh with pain, but she mistook the cause.

She turned from him and again faced Damont. "You two are acting like beasts, not men," she blazed, dashing the tears from her eyes. "I've been told that I was the cause of this and I shall hold myself responsible if this duel is fought. You've both professed to love me and you've both asked me to marry you. What a poor way for you to show your love! If you think that this will help either of you, you're mistaken. I could never marry a murderer; so if you meant what you said, you'll not go on with this."

"Mademoiselle, you're taking unfair advantage of these two men," interrupted the referee. "And this is a most unbecoming situation for a woman to be in. This is a man's affair. Please let us settle it in the customary way."

"I'll do nothing of the kind!" she retorted. "It is they who are taking an unfair advantage of me. I'd be responsible for the death of one of them. If you won't promise to call this off, then I'll stay here until we all drop from fatigue. And if you dare to raise those swords again, I'll stand between you, and your sword point will have to go through my body before it reaches either one of you."

Damont saw an opportunity to bring this unpleasant situation to an end. He didn't want the fight in the first place and now he was willing to call it off and perhaps win her favor in doing so.

"I'm willing to forget the insult my opponent gave

me," he said, "if he is willing to forget it. I call these as witnesses that I am willing to cross swords and then stop the fight if he is."

"That's wonderful!" she exclaimed. "It is very generous of you." She turned to Chenier. "What do you say, Monsieur?"

He hesitated a moment, than said, doggedly, "I'd rather settle this with my fists. But he's afraid." He charged as his doubled fist swept the air.

She gazed at him a moment with a look he had never seen in her eyes before, a look of hurt, a pleading, a something which made his heart beat faster and which gave him a faint glimmer of hope. A step nearer she came and asked in tones which he alone could hear, "Would you degrade me by fighting like that?"

"No. I couldn't," he said slowly. A feeling, never experienced before, of defilement and shame, perhaps humility, made his reply curt. "All right, Damont, we'll cross swords and call it quits."

"And if you don't stop then, I shall be there between those two points," she warned.

"Don't you trust me?" Damont asked reproachfully.

"No, I don't," she retorted. "Not until this is over with and I have your promise that it won't be renewed at some future time."

The referee, with as much dignity as he could muster, gave the signal for them to again take position and then repeated the words which would have been the signal for them to begin the fight. They raised their weapons, advanced the points and let them touch, then lowered the points to the ground as a signal that the affair was ended.

"Thank you so much, Monsieur, for being so generous," Elise cried, grasping Damont's hand and kissing it. Then she turned to Chenier. "Do I have your solemn pledge, in the presence of these witnesses that you'll never try to resume this duel?"

"You have mine," Damont assured her.

She turned to Chenier. "What do you say, Monsieur?"

"You know what the answer is," he said. "I won't fight him." He was angry and hurt that she had kissed Damont's hand and had ignored him. He couldn't know that it was in gratitude to Damont for saving his life.

"Now shall we go?" the referee suggested. He was disgusted at the outcome of the affair. This was not according to custom.

"May I walk home with you?" Damont asked as he prepared to leave.

"No. I shall go as I came, alone," she told him. "You men go first. I shall follow. I shall stay here a little while and — and — thank God that He has answered prayer."

They left her and started toward town. As they reached a bend in the road, Chenier turned and looked back to where they had left her. She was kneeling at the foot of one of the oaks, with her face uplifted and her lips parted in prayer. He knew, as he slowly turned away, that he would carry that picture in his memory as long as he lived. It did something to him which all her pleadings and all her talking about God had never done. Perhaps that had been the seed sowing which brought forth the harvest, but it broke down the cold wall of resistance within his heart. He realized that her prayer and her pleadings had saved his life and he knew in that moment as he saw her there upon her knees with tear-wet face uplifted, that if he had gone out into eternity he would have indeed been a lost soul.

Something came to him like showers upon the mown grass, melting away the hard shell of doubt and unbelief within his heart. When he reached his room he threw himself upon his knees and did something which he had never done since he was a little fellow. He cried aloud as great sobs shook him.

He began in a halting, stumbling voice to pray something he had never done in his life. "God, I don't know how to talk to You," he said, "but I want what she's got. I want to believe as she does. I want to have the assurance that she has that I'm forgiven and that it's all right between You and me. I know I'm a sinner, but she says You can forgive me. Do it now, God! Please do it now!"

After a time the sobs ceased and a sense of peace and calm came to him, a new sense of inward peace that he had never known before. As he rose from his knees and went to wash his face he spoke aloud to himself.

"This must be it," he said. "This must be what she said would happen. This must be the peace that passeth understanding."

CHAPTER 18

News of the duel became known to only a few. The fact that there had really been no fight robbed it of any interest it might have had for those who loved to gossip about such things. Those who had been witnesses to the unusual end to the expected fight said nothing about Elise's appearance on the scene. This beautiful girl had created a respect for her that forbade them talking about it to anyone. They knew that if her name were coupled with the affair, she would be submitted to some unpleasant publicity.

Damont was much pleased at the outcome of the affair. He knew that what he had done would win Elise's gratitude and he was determined to use that to his advantage if possible. There still remained the fear that Rosalie would do something to bring an end to his hopes, or that White Dove would appear again and reveal a truth which would most surely blast his hopes forever. Chenier still remained upon the scene and that gave him no end of annoyance. His one hope was that he might be able to think up something that would make her think less of Chenier, and so leave the way open to him.

That afternoon he went to the Market Place and

bought a basket of provisions and took them to Madame Romain's. Elise was not there when he came, so he chatted with the old lady until she came in, laden with bundles of sewing brought from two of her customers.

"I've done a very presumptuous thing," he said. "I've invited myself to dine with you and I've brought the dinner with me. It only needs the magic of your touch to transform it into an appetizing meal. Do you mind? It's been so long since you've invited me."

"No, indeed," she replied. "I would have been glad to have you without your furnishing the meal, though it might not have been quite so bountiful. My goodness!" she exclaimed as she eyed the contents of the basket. "We'll never be able to eat all of that, even if I could cook it all at one time."

"Perhaps you'll let me come back again and finish it," he said, smiling. "I've waited so long for an invitation. You seem to have forgotten how much I enjoy coming here for a meal."

"I've been so busy sewing that I haven't had time to think of much else since the fever," she confessed. "Madame and I have been living on snacks. It will be fun to cook a real meal once more. And of course we shall be glad to have you enjoy it with us."

Nothing was said about the duel during the meal for Madame knew nothing about it; but when the dishes had been stacked and they had gone outside, Elise said, "Monsieur Damont, I've been wanting all evening to tell you how grateful I am to you for not going on with that fight. I never would have gotten over it if either one of you had been killed or injured."

"I didn't want to fight in the first place," he told her. "But Chenier placed me in such a position that I couldn't refuse to accept his challenge. He lost his head and accused me of a terrible thing in the presence of the Governor. For your sake, if for no other reason, I didn't want to fight him, but Bienville as good as told me that I should accept the challenge."

"Was my name brought into it?" she asked.

"Yes, he admitted with seeming reluctance.

"Why?"

"I'd rather not tell you," he said. "It was a lie." He saw an opportunity to put Chenier in an unpleasant a light as possible.

"I think I have a right to know, since my name was brought into it," she insisted.

"He accused me of trying to have him murdered because I was in love with you and wanted him out of the way."

"Oh no!" she exclaimed. "I'm sure he couldn't accuse you of a thing like that. How could he have thought such a thing?"

"Because, for one thing, he's hot-headed. The first time he saw you on the ship he wanted me to keep away from you or he'd fight me. He wanted to fight me that first day, and he's been looking for an excuse to fight me ever since."

"But to accuse you of trying to have him murdered! That doesn't make sense. Where did he get such an idea?"

"His jealousy made him imagine it, I suppose. It seems that some renegade tried to shoot him when he was on his way to the Punica settlement. He killed the fellow and left his body in the woods. When he came back to make his report to Bienville he accused me of sending the fellow after him to murder him. He said I wanted to get him out of the way because we were both in love with you."

"How terrible!"

A silence fell between them. She could think of nothing but that Chenier had killed a man and laid the blame for that killing upon Damont. That is, if Damont's story was true. She wondered just how much truth there was in what he said. The feeling she had had for so long, inspired by the ruthless purpose which seemed to lie behind that friendly exterior, which unwittingly gleamed through those cold eyes of his, came to her again, making her doubt that he was telling her the whole truth. That there was some truth in his account of the affair she was forced to believe, for he knew that she could verify what he had told her. She was anxious to hear Chenier tell his side of the story. The thought of the killing was uppermost in her mind, however. That was one thing that Andre would have to explain. To him it might be only an incident in a wild and reckless life, but to her it was a terrible thing. It would be just one more barrier to the love which seemed to grow stronger within her heart in spite of her effort to destroy it. She must wait until she could talk with Andre before she passed judgment upon him.

"Why are you so silent?" Damont asked presently while he watched the play of emotions upon her lovely face.

"I was just thinking of how complicated life is and of how little people seem to value the worth of an immortal soul."

"Life is complicated," he admitted. "We struggle for wealth and power, and when wealth is achieved we realize that there is no real joy in achievement. Then someone comes along who is the answer to every dream and desire a man could have. His whole aim in life is to win that one, but she seems just beyond his reach. That really complicates life, doesn't it?"

She answered his smile, but there was no smile in her heart, only unrest and anxiety. She wanted most of all to talk to Andre.

Andre Chenier had come to see her while they were eating. He had seen Damont inside and had gone away disappointed. He had been eager to tell her what had happened to him, eager to know what her reaction would be. He knew that she would rejoice with him in his new-found salvation, but he was hoping that that joy would not be wholly impersonal. The one great barrier that had stood between them was now removed. If she would only believe that his salvation was real, as real as he knew it to be; then perhaps one day his great love for her might awaken a responding love within her heart. He was happier than he had ever been before, happy because of the new peace within his heart, happy in the hope that was his. The sight of Damont sitting by Elise, talking with her easily and smoothly, was like a dash of cold water upon his hopes. Damont was still to be reckoned with. He had done everything possible to ingratiate himself into Elise's favor. Now that he looked at life differently, he knew that he could not fight Damont again, no matter what Damont might do to provoke him. Young as he was in his faith, he knew that in the future nothing could be settled in that way.

Upon his return from the cottage he received another summons from Bienville and hastened to the Governor's home.

"I've sent for you to go upon another mission," Bienville began, "but this time I assure you that there will be no grounds for you to make charges of ambush and murder. I'm sending you with men I have picked, to lead them to the spot where you claim Laclede's body was left. If there is enough evidence to prove your story true, we shall see what steps to take. If the body cannot be found, then we shall be forced to let the matter drop and you can apologize to Monsieur Damont. As long as I am governor of the colony I shall endeavor to see that justice is administered without fear or favor."

"I shall be glad to help search for the body,"

Chenier assured him. "But I doubt if anything can be found except possibly a few bones. If the skull can be found, you shall at least know that I was telling the truth about Laclede's death. As for my accusations against Damont, we'll let that drop. That was settled between us this morning."

Chenier was surprised at the calmness of his own voice. Strange that there was no more hatred in his heart for Damont in spite of his suspicions about the affair of Laclede. Surely this must be what Elise had told him and what he had doubted and secretly scoffed at. This was what she had called the new birth. He was beyond a doubt a new creature in Christ Jesus. The realization thrilled him.

"You fought the duel, I suppose. Did you kill him?" Bienville's face became grim and stern.

Chenier shook his head. "No. We crossed swords and ended it without fighting. We both agreed that the matter was settled."

"H'm! A miracle must have happened to bring about such an end as that," the governor commented.

"A miracle did happen, but I'm not at liberty to say what it was. But that's over with. Just let me go and try to find the body and clear my name of murder. If that is done, that's all I ask."

Early the next morning they set out upon the trail. He was impatient to get the trip over with. It would be a few days before he could get to see Elise, and just now days would seem like years. Little did he know all that would happen before he got to tell her what he longed to have her know.

CHAPTER 19

Elise went to see Annette as soon as she could the next afternoon. She wanted to tell her what had happened and to thank her again for letting her know about the duel. She had a dress to fit, and while she worked they talked. Then Annette suggested that they go out to the berry patch not far from the house.

The small farm on the outskirts of the town was surrounded on two sides by the woods. Just on the edge of these woods there were berries ripening. As they picked berries they wandered farther and farther into the woods, not realizing how far they were from the house. Since the massacre at Fort Rosalie, Annette had never ventured far into the woods, for no one ever knew when a stray savage might be prowling about. There was little to fear from the nearby, friendly Chouachas, but lately it had been rumored that wandering Indians from the still vengeful Punicas had been seen near the town.

The girls were busy picking berries and talking, or perhaps they would have heard the stealthy approach of one of the Punicas. This fellow had lost all his family when the soldiers came to the rescue of the settlement, and he was bent upon taking vengeance. Neither one of them saw his dark painted form approach, until Elise, warned by some inner voice looked up and with horrified eyes she saw him about to strike a knife into Annette's back as she bent over a berry bush. With a scream of warning she threw herself between the savage and his intended victim. The sudden scream and her unexpected rush to Annette's defense took the savage by surprise, otherwise she might have been killed instantly. It fell upon Elise, striking her shoulder, but with the force of the blow lessened.

At her scream Annette turned. She too uttered a scream as Elise fell, and she threw her bucket full into the face of the vicious looking assailant. She acted upon sheer impulse, but it was the thing which saved their lives, for the Indian, blinded by the pain of the blow from the heavily laden bucket, fled into the woods and disappeared.

Annette knelt by Elise's side and saw that blood was flowing freely from the wound in her shoulder. Annette could see that the wound was deep and she knew it was dangerous. Elise had been stunned by the blow and by her fall and Annette didn't know what to do. She was afraid to leave her lying there while she ran for help, and she was afraid to try to drag Elise nearer the house for fear that she might open the wound more. While she was debating what to do, Elise opened her eyes and tried to get up. She moaned and lay back again while she put her hand to her shoulder. It was wet with blood.

"I can't move," she moaned. "Go and get help."

"I'm afraid to leave you here," Annette cried.

She ran a little distance down the trail toward the house, screaming for help. One of Boudreaux's workmen heard her and came running to her. She told him what had happened.

"You stay here with her while I go for help," she told him and flew as fast as she could toward town.

She had not gone far when she met Damont. He

was looking for Monsieur Boudreaux about some work. She called frantically to him.

"Elise has been hurt. Come and help us. I'm afraid she will die."

As they hurried back to Elise, Annette told him what had happened.

"If she dies, I'll never get over it," Annette sobbed. "She took the blow that was meant for me. If she hadn't, I'd be dead now, for that Indian was right upon us before either of us saw him."

Damont didn't answer. He was too much perturbed. The thought of Elise dying brought chaos to his thoughts.

When they came to where she lay, Damont knelt down beside her, and did what he could to stop the flow of blood. Then he told the workman to get Dr. Norris, the only physician in the colony since the fever epidemic.

As the workman ran to notify the doctor, Damont spoke to Annette. "Let's get her to the house," he said, tying the crude tourniquet a little tighter he picked her up, and carried her to the house.

Annette went ahead to prepare a bed for her. Then they waited anxiously for the doctor.

By the time he arrived, Elise had recovered from the shock enough to talk. "I'll be all right," she said. "Don't worry. But my shoulder and arm hurt terribly."

"No wonder," Damont told her. "You've got an ugly gash there that goes part way down your arm. Here's the doctor now. He'll get you fixed up and more comfortable before long."

The doctor cut her dress off her shoulder and looked at the wound.

"It's a miracle that the muscles weren't severed," he remarked as he prepared to dress the wound. "That tourniquet helped to save her life. She couldn't stand to lose any more blood. I'll have to take some stiches, and that's going to hurt plenty," he told Elise. "Try to stand it. You're lucky to be alive."

"I can stand it," she assured him.

When the sutures were being made the pain was excruciating. Elise pressed her lips together in an effort to keep from groaning, but occasionally the pain was more than she could bear silently and a faint moan escaped her pale lips. Finally the ordeal was over, and the doctor suggested that a little brandy be given her to strengthen her.

"Won't black coffee do just as well?" she asked. "I don't want brandy."

"I have some coffee on the stove now," Annette said. "I'll heat it up for you," and went into the kitchen.

"She doesn't drink liquor," Damont told the doctor.

The doctor went on to say, "It's a question whether or not her constitution is strong enough to withstand the shock and the loss of blood. The next day or so will tell the tale."

Damont raised a warning hand to the doctor. He didn't want Elise frightened.

"Nonsense," the doctor replied in answer to the warning. "I think it's always best for the patient to know the truth. If they're going to die, they ought to know it."

Elise smiled faintly through pallid lips. "I'm not afraid to die," she told him. "If it's the Lord's will, I'm ready to go."

Annette came with the coffee. Elise drank, then closed her eyes and lay back with a sigh. "Who will take care of Madame now?" she murmured.

"I shall take care of you both," Damont stated. "I'll get my carriage and put you on the back seat and take you home with me. Madame can come and be there with you until you're well enough to go home again."

"Why can't she stay here?" Annette asked. "I'd be glad to take care of her. I'll never be able to repay her for what she did for me."

"It's better for her to be where she can have every attention. Madame can be with her and keep her company, and my servants can take care of her needs. She will need plenty of nourishment and I shall see that she gets everything she needs."

Elise demurred. "I can't let you do that."

Damont leaned over and smiled at her. "This is one time you can't have anything to say about it. When you're well again, you can invite me to dinner. This is just what one friend would do for another in time of need. Won't you look at it that way? I promise you that I shall look at it that way."

She nodded, too weak for the effort of speech.

"Thanks. Then that's settled." He turned to the doctor. "Will it be all right if she is put on a stretcher and handled carefully?"

"Just so long as you don't do anything to open that wound again."

He left some medicine and said he would call at Damont's that evening.

Scarcely conscious of what was being done, Elise was put into one of the huge, four posted beds in Damont's bachelor home. The thick soft mattress felt restful to her aching body, and in a few minutes she was asleep. Madame Romain was sent for, and much perturbed, took her vigil by the girl's bedside.

During the next two days the anxious watchers waited to see whether Elise would win the battle against loss of blood, shock and possible infection from the vicious wound. They were thankful when the doctor told them that so far as he could tell, the danger from infection had passed. She had developed no serious symptoms, and it only remained to be seen whether she would withstand the loss of blood.

Damont came at frequent intervals and stood beside the bed. He did not speak to her often, for she slept most of the time between hours of taking nourishment; but if she were awake, he would press her hand gently and smile down into her eyes. He had never been so miserable in his whole life. Not until now, when he faced the possibility of losing her through death did he realize how essential she was to his very life. Without her he wouldn't want to go on. Never in all his misspent life had he ever loved anyone with an unselfish love, and this new experience was in danger of bringing to him a greater sorrow than he had thought life could hold for him. He had never before faced sorrow. His parents had died before he knew the real meaning of sorrow, and his whole life had been spent in the attaining of his own desires. Now he began to know what sorrow could really mean, and he wasn't prepared to face it. He moved restlessly about the house, unwilling to leave until he should know whether or not she would live. The thought of giving her up to Chenier had never filled him with such fear as he faced now. He had determined that Chenier should never have her, but in the face of this other rival — death — he was helpless and terrified.

Madame hobbled about the house, her dim old eyes filled with tears, in the brief moments when she left Elise's side. Often she would kneel by the bed and pray earnestly for the girl's life to be spared. She had learned the secret and the power of prayer in the short time since she had been saved, and it was the only thing which gave her comfort and hope in this dark hour. She tried to do as Elise had so often told her, to cast her burden upon the Lord and to look to Him to sustain her in time of stress and anxiety. Now she was learning this, and she was amazed at the sense of peace which came to her heart even though the tears might overflow her eyes. She had met the Source of all comfort.

Annette was perhaps the most miserable of the three. It was for her life that Elise had brought this upon herself and she couldn't get away from that thought. Elise had told her once that there was no greater love than that of one who would lay down his life for his friends. She had tried to tell Annette how Christ had laid down His life for her because He loved her and didn't want to see her lost, but she had refused to let her talk very much about it. Even after the fever epidemic when Claire had died, she had refused to listen. But the words had been there in the back of her mind all this time, waiting for God's promise to be fulfilled that they would not return unto Him void.

Now they came to her in a rush of remembrance. She realized what had prompted Elise to do this thing, to save her life at the risk of her own. It was the same reason which had prompted Elise to come to her during the fever and risk her life by caring for her and her husband. She realized, with an overwhelming sense of guilt, her unworthiness and her sin before the God whom she had spurned and whom she had mocked so many times. She longed to come to Him and tell Him how sorry she was and how unworthy she was to receive anything from Him. But she felt that she had passed beyond the limit of His forgiveness.

Never before had she felt this desire, but now it took possession of her, robbing her of sleep and making her haunt the house where Elise lay facing death which had no terrors for her. Annette remembered the storm and Elise's calm in the face of it. What if that Indian had succeeded in striking her with that knife? She would be — she shuddered at a word which she had so often flippantly used — she would now be in hell.

She had scoffed at the idea of hell, but now she faced it in the light of what might have happened and she knew that what Elise had told her was true, that there was a heaven for the redeemed and hell for those who refused the only way of salvation, the shed blood of Christ applied to the heart of a penitent sinner.

When she could stand the strain of desire and fear no longer, she went to Elise. She had not tried to talk to her before, for every time she tried to say a word she felt the tears come and she didn't want to upset Elise by tears. Now she had to talk to her, if Damont said she might.

Damont had just received the good news from the doctor that he thought Elise was passing the crisis and that she would live, though it would take some time for her to get her strength back. He told Annette that she might talk to Elise.

Elise greeted her with a smile. She looked stronger today than she had since the attack. Annette's heart was thrilled with joy to know that she would live.

"How can I ever repay you for what you did for me?" she began. "You were willing to die for me and I'm not worth it. All my life I'll be in your debt, for every breath I breathe will belong to you."

"No," Elise contradicted. "Every breath you breathe comes from God. Every good and perfect gift comes from Him. You don't owe me anything, but you owe Him everything, for He died to save your soul."

Annette's lips were trembling and there were tears in her eyes. Elise had never seen her in this mood before. Hope brought a faint color to her cheek.

"That's what I want to talk to you about," Annette blurted out. "Elise, I want what you've got, but I'm afraid it's too late for me to ask for it. I've wanted to, but I don't know how and I'm afraid I've put it off too long. Do you think there's any hope for someone as mean and low as I?"

"Of course there is. Jesus said, 'Behold I stand at the door and knock.' If He wasn't knocking at your door you wouldn't want to be saved. He said 'If any man hear my voice and open the door, I will come in to him, and will sup with him, and he with me.' Open the door, Annette, and let Him in."

She laid one frail hand upon Annette's bowed head, and prayed that Annette might receive the blessed gift of eternal life. Presently Annette's voice joined hers as she told the Lord what a sinner she was and how she longed to have pardon and redemption. When she raised her tearstained face there was peace and a new light in the eyes which had been so hard and so scoffing.

"God has forgiven you, dear," Elise said while tears of happiness filled her own eyes. "Do you believe God has done what He said He would do?"

Annette nodded while she wiped her eyes. "Yes, I understand now what you meant. What a fool I was not to have listened to you long ago!"

"If it took this to make you accept the Lord, then I'm glad it happened, even though I've been such a burden to everyone."

Madame had come into the room, though they had not noticed her. She had prayed along with the girls. "You haven't been a burden to anyone," she said. "God must have brought you here to New Orleans so that we could be saved. You've been a blessing to us all, not a burden."

"I was thinking of a verse that I took as my promise when we were first captured and brought here," Elise said. " 'In the way of righteousness is life and in the pathway thereof there is no death.' God leads us over strange pathways sometimes, but there is always a purpose in His leading. I'm glad He brought me here."

CHAPTER 20

Rosalie Allain had finally heard a garbled account of the duel. She did not know the name of Damont's opponent and was not interested in knowing it. She had met Chenier at the governor's reception but she had forgotten him, for her thoughts that night were centered upon Damont and Elise. The one thing which interested her now was the fact that Damont cared enough for Elise to fight a duel because of her. The rumors which reached her gave no cause for the duel, only that there was some girl connected with the fight which had ended without the shedding of blood.

She felt that it was time for her to do something about this love affair of the man she had marked for her own. When the news of the Indian's attack and of the care Elise was receiving in Damont's home became known to her, it made her desperate to do something to kill the romance. It had never occurred to her that Elise was not in love with Damont. He had everything a girl could desire — wealth, position and handsome appearance. He would prove attractive to any girl seeking a husband, and she believed that such was Elise's object, in spite of Elise's denials on the occasions when Rosalie had indirectly discussed the subject with her.

She decided she'd go to see Elise. She prepared a basket of fruit, cookies and preserves and went to Damont's. She knew that he would not like the idea of her seeing Elise, but she also knew that there was nothing he could do about it. He dared not refuse to let her see Elise. On her first visit, Elise was too weak to talk much, but she found that Elise was grateful for the visit and the delicacies. She was asked to come again. This Rosalie had already decided to do. She wanted to see the girl when Damont was not there.

She bided her time until Elise grew stronger and was able to sit up. Damont, relieved of the anxiety, went to his office for a while each day and Madame took time out for her usual afternoon nap. Rosalie, by a system of espionage which she would have scorned to use for any other purpose, found this out and timed her visit with this knowledge. She rejoiced at her good fortune when she found Elise alone.

This time, as on her other visits, she brought the girl a little gift, cookies and fruit and some pralines.

"You've been so good to me," Elise told Rosalie as she set the basket down. "I don't deserve such good treatment."

"I haven't brought it because you deserve it, my dear," Rosalie said in her most honeyed voice, "but because I've grown very fond of you and I want to see you get well and to be happy again."

"I'm almost well and I shall soon be able to get back to work. That will make me very happy, for I feel that I've been such a bother to Monsieur Damont."

"He has been most kind, hasn't he," Rosalie remarked, but the sarcasm was not apparent to Elise.

"Yes, he has. He's been more than a friend and he's done more than I'd ever expect a friend to do.

He's been wonderful, and I shall always be grateful. I shall feel that, in a measure, I owe my life to him."

"That's only natural," Rosalie agreed. "I suppose I should feel that way too if I were in your place," and then she changed the subject.

They talked of other things for a while, while Rosalie planned just how she would release her poisoned barb. She wanted to wait until she was ready to leave before she did so.

Finally she rose and said she must be going. "I shall come again soon, but I don't want to tire you out this time." She hesitated a moment, then said with a note of reluctance in her voice, "My dear, I feel that I must tell you something which may cause you pain, but I think you ought to know. It's better to suffer now, than to suffer much more later on. If I didn't know what your ideas are about so many things I'd never say a word."

"What is it?" asked Elise, alarmed by the seriousness in the other's voice. "Tell me, if you think I should know."

"Perhaps I shouldn't tell you, I hate to say it, but your beloved Andre has no right to your love. At least not by your standards. He has an Indian wife. He married her before you came here. I've known it all along, but I hated to tell you. Believe me, I did."

Elise was silent. She looked at her visitor with eyes that told Rosalie that the barb had done its work. "I can't believe it," she finally managed to say.

Rosalie shrugged. "Don't believe it if you don't want to. Perhaps it won't make any difference to you after all. We haven't been too particular about these things here in the colony. But I thought you should know. What you do about it is up to you."

"Thank you for telling me," Elsie stammered.

Rosalie congratulated herself upon her cleverness in letting the barb fly. She knew that Elise would never marry Damont with that knowledge. She knew her well enough to know that she would spurn his love, no matter how grateful she might feel for what he had done for her. But Rosalie would have been aghast if she had known the unexpected twist her scheme had taken.

Back in the room Elise was lying shocked and stricken. The knowledge left her so shaken that she felt as if all her world had suddenly collapsed, leaving her in a whirlpool of suffering and despair. When Rosalie had told her that "her beloved Andre" was married to an Indian girl, she never once thought of Damont. She had never called him Andre and the fact that both his and Chenier's given names were the same never once entered her thoughts now. To her, there was but one Andre. Somehow Madame Allain had discovered her love for Andre and in her kindness was warning her before she yielded to that love and married him.

Perhaps if she had been stronger she might have reasoned the thing out and realized that Rosalie could not have meant the Andre whom she loved, but in this hour of shock she couldn't reason; she could only feel the pain which this hideous knowledge left within her heart.

Not long afterwards Damont returned and he saw that something had happened. She looked so stricken and her face was all tear stained.

"What's the matter?" he cried in alarm and knelt beside the bed. "My dearest, what has happened to make you like this? Has the wound started paining you again?"

She turned her tear-filled eyes upon his anxious face and said hesitatingly, "Not that wound — but — something deeper. Madame Allain was here and told me something that I find it almost impossible to believe."

Damont's heart contracted with sudden fear. "What did she tell you?" he managed to ask.

"She told me that — that — Andre was married to an Indian girl. She said he had married her before I came here." Tears trickled down her face and she did not try to wipe them off.

He was overwhelmed with the strange twist that events had taken. How had Rosalie found out about his marriage to White Dove? She couldn't possibly know about this marriage. No one knew that but him. Yet she must have known, or she wouldn't have told this to Elise. She had done this because she thought Elise was in love with him, Damont. He determined to use this strange confusion to his advantage if he could.

"You love Chenier, don't you?" he asked sadly.

"No, I don't!" she cried with a sudden surge of strength. He saw in that very vehemence the truth that she denied. "I have nothing but contempt for him now. I trusted him as a friend and while I was trusting him he was trying to win my love and persuade me to marry him when he had no right to do either. How could he have been so low! I never want to see him again."

"I'm sorry if you have been hurt," he said tenderly. "My one desire is that you should always be happy."

"Thank you," and she gave him a wan smile. "You've been so wonderful to me. Do you really think — believe — that he is married? Do you really think it is true?"

"I couldn't tell you that," he evaded. "But I know that many of the *coureurs de bois* do have Indian wives. They don't regard that as any barrier to another marriage. They don't look upon that as real marriage."

"But in the sight of God it is," she replied. "How could he do this to me?"

"Because he loved you so much, I suppose," he answered. "I can understand how he would feel. Don't judge him too harshly. You have no idea how desirable you are and how much a man could love you."

"I'm not judging him," she said slowly. "God will do that. But I just don't want to see him again."

After Damont had left her, she lay there for a long time too stricken to do anything but suffer. She couldn't think; she couldn't pray. When finally the storm of weeping came it helped to ease the tension and the shock. At last she drifted into the sleep of exhaustion. When she wakened she poured out the burden of her heart to the One who had never failed her. Even in despair there was peace within her heart, for she knew that God would give her strength to go on with a life which had suddenly seemed so empty.

Chenier had been longer on his search than he had anticipated. When his party reached the spot where he had left Laclede's body there was no trace of it. Evidently it had been carried away by some animal to its lair. It had rained since he had been on the trail, and any signs of the body having been dragged away were obliterated. They searched in every direction, Chenier frantically trying to find the only evidence that would clear him in his accusations against Damont and satisfy the governor that he had not concocted the whole story. Their search was fruitless, however, and he finally returned, much disappointed and worried. His one hope of clearing his name had disappeared completely.

Bienville received the report of the group with a shrug of his shoulders and a meaningful glance at Chenier.

"If there is no body, then there can be no proof of either murder or a plot to murder you," he said significantly. "I'd advise you that the next time you make such a charge, Monsieur, that you bring the body back with you. Then the proof will not be lacking."

At another time Chenier would have lost his temper and maintained the truth of the charges he had made; but a change had taken place within him and though he smarted under the governor's words, he was silent, a reaction which surprised himself as much as it did the governor.

He was eager to see Elise, and went to the cottage as soon as he had left the governor. The place was deserted. Much surprised and not a little worried, he went to see Annette. She told him what had happened and gave him the encouraging news that Elise was out of danger. He hated to have to go to Damont's home, but he went there and asked to see her. Damont greeted him with the message Elise had given him.

"She said she didn't want to see you again," he told the astonished Chenier.

"I don't believe it," Chenier retorted. "You're just trying to keep me from seeing her." He tried to control his anger, but he felt it rising within him. There was such smug satisfaction written upon Damont's every feature.

"Wait here a minute and I'll let someone else prove that I'm telling you the truth," and he went inside and got Madame. She came to the door and stared at Chenier with eyes that had lost their friendliness.

"Tell Monsieur what Mademoiselle Elise said to you," he told her. "He won't believe me when I say that she doesn't want to see him."

"It's true, Monsieur," said the old lady sadly. "I don't know what's happened to her, but she said that I should tell you she didn't want to ever see you again."

"What have you two done to her, that she can't even be friends with me any more?" Chenier asked helplessly.

"Nothing, I assure you," Damont told him. "I've only tried to save her life when she needed someone who could give her the attention she needed. What has happened is between you and her."

There was nothing left for Chenier to do but leave. He went to see Annette again, but she could give him no clue to Elise's strange behavior. He went home, disconsolate and angry. Why did this have to happen just when he had been so sure that everything was going to be so wonderful? He hadn't yet learned to take his problems to the Lord, so he fumed and fretted and grew more morose and upset with each passing day. When a company of immigrants came on the next ship and needed a guide to take them to the lands they were supposed to occupy, he welcomed the opportunity for some action and agreed to guide them to the new settlements. He knew that it would be useless to try to see Elise until she and Madame returned to the cottage. The trip would give him something to do until that time. He was determined to get at the truth of this strange change in her, but he could only bide his time and hope for the best.

CHAPTER 21

Elise and Madame returned to the cottage, and Elise took up her duties against the doctor's advice and the pleas of Damont. She felt that she couldn't be dependent upon him any longer and she had to get to work, for she hoped that it would help her to forget the ache in her heart.

She had not realized until now how completely her love for Chenier had filled her life. It had given her something wonderful to anticipate, for she was living in the assurance that one day he would give his heart to her Lord and that then she might let him know how much she loved him. It had been this bright hope that had filled the drab days with the sunshine of promise, which had taken away weariness and hardship from long tedious hours of work.

Now there was nothing left but pain and disappointment and anger against him for having won her love when he had no right to it. She tried to overcome that love and to forget him, but she found that the more she tried to forget, the stronger grew the memory. She assumed a cheerfulness which did not deceive Madame. The old lady grieved over the mystery of this sudden change toward Chenier. She had secretly hoped that Elise would one day marry

Chenier, for, in spite of Damont's kindness, she preferred Chenier, and she had thought that Elise did also. She asked Elise why she had changed so suddenly, but Elise refused to tell her.

Andre Damont was in a fever of impatience to bend Elise to his desire to marry her. He knew that his good fortune couldn't last long and that sooner or later she would find out the truth about what Rosalie had told her. He was glad that Chenier was out of the way for a while, for it gave him a little more time. There was one desperate hope which he clung to, yet which he feared to see realized. He was not sure whether it would drive Elise to him or whether she would be farther from him than ever. It was the edict which had been pending for some time and which as yet Bienville had not put into effect.

There had come to the colony another group of immigrants. In this group there were some of good German stock, some less desirable settlers and a number of unmarried women who were utterly immoral, reducing the already low state of the colony to a lower depth. It had been suggested that the governor issue an edict forbidding any unmarried girl to remain in the colony. This was to be the last resort. One of the older customs had had little effect upon these wildly reckless new-comers. That custom had been tried in the earlier days of the settlement with satisfactory results. When a woman was found to be flagrantly immoral, she was publicly strapped to a wooden horse in the *Place d' Armes* and whipped by the soldiers. These new-comers, however, defied the whippings, openly naming their partners in sin while they were being flogged. For obvious reasons this practice was not continued.

Damont learned from Bienville that he was planning to publish the edict soon. He went to see Elise as soon as he learned this. He was anxious to know how she would react. He was hoping for the best, yet he feared that his hopes would be destroyed.

She was still much thinner, but she had regained her strength surprisingly fast and the color had come back to her cheeks. She greeted him with a cordial word of welcome.

"I was wondering how long you were going to keep me waiting to pay back some of your hospitality."

"I didn't come to collect any debts," he smiled, "but just to see how you're getting along."

"But you will stay for dinner, won't you? A whiff of that gumbo I've just cooked and that apple pie ought to persuade you, even if I can't."

"I feel myself yielding to temptation," he said as he sat upon the step.

After dinner the three of them sat outside for a while in the gathering dusk, then Madame went inside and left them alone.

"Monsieur Damont," Elise began, "I never can repay you for what you have done for me, but I want to tell you again how grateful I am and how much I do thank you. I shall feel under obligation to you all my life."

"I wouldn't want you to marry me, Elise, because of any sense of obligation you might have, but I'm just wondering if my love for you had made any change in your feelings toward me. Are you learning to love me, or is there hope that you might learn?"

"I'm sorry, terribly sorry, but I haven't changed. I wish I could tell you that I love you, but I can't."

"I'm more sorry than you are," he said with a new note of seriousness in his voice. "Sorry for you as well as for myself. Something is coming up that will make life very difficult for you, unless you love someone else enough to marry him."

"What do you mean?" she asked in surprise.

"I've just learned that Bienville is about to issue an

edict which he's been considering for some time. The edict is that every girl of marriageable age in the colony shall marry. If this law is put into force, then all these creatures who have come here recently will either marry and settle down to be decent citizens, or else get out. I have an idea that they will marry, for they don't have any money for transportation back to where they came from."

She was visibly astonished. "That means me too, doesn't it?"

"Yes. That is why I was hoping that you cared enough for me to marry me. I wish there was something I could do to get you some sort of special dispensation, but if the edict goes through, you'll face the same alternatives as the others."

"Then I shall have to leave the colony," she said slowly.

"How could you leave? Where would you go?"

"I don't know. I haven't any idea."

"Oh, Elise, why don't you marry me? You couldn't leave here. You know that. Give me a chance to try to make you happy. I could make you happy even if you didn't love me. Won't you give me a chance?" There was a note of desperation in his voice that brought pity to her heart. She knew from her own experience, just what he must feel.

"It isn't a question of my own happiness, Monsieur, but of doing God's will," she said. "I couldn't marry you, even if I dared to without loving you, for you're not a Christian."

"I'll be a Christian, the kind of Christian you demand in a husband, if you'll marry me," he said earnestly. "Tell me what I must do to be one and I'll do it. I love you enough to be anything you want me to be."

"You don't become a Christian that way," she said with a smile. "You don't just make up your mind you're going to be one and then become one. You have to realize that you're a sinner and you have to want Him to save you, above everything else, for your own sake, not to please me or because of anyone else but Him. And you can never realize your need of salvation unless the Holy Spirit puts the consciousness of your need within your heart."

He felt that it would be useless to pursue that line of argument any further just now. He thought of Chenier and a sense of relief swept over him. Chenier couldn't meet this standard of hers any more than he could. He'd best let matters stand for the present, but he couldn't wait long. Too many things might happen to frustrate his plans and hopes.

"This is a serious situation, my dear," he said. "Think it over, won't you, and try to forget some of the standards you've set for yourself. If this edict is issued, you'll be forced to do something about it and you know you can't leave here. What could you do but obey the edict?"

"I don't know," she said in sombre tones, "but I know that God will provide a way for me. He has never failed me yet."

On his way home, Damont cursed what he called this prudish idea of hers; he cursed the forces which seemed arrayed against him; and he cursed himself for being such a fool as to want her when wanting her was causing him so much unrest. But he was more doggedly determined than ever to have her, no matter what obstacles might intervene.

Chenier eventually returned and again tried to see Elise, but she saw him coming and sent Madame to meet him. "Tell him that I don't want to see him," she said, "and ask him please not to come here again."

Madame delivered the message and though he insisted and argued with the old lady, she was adamant and would not let him in.

"Won't she even tell me why she doesn't want to see me?" he begged, when he saw that arguments didn't avail.

"Perhaps, some day," the old lady replied. "I don't know myself what her reason is, but it's a good one or she wouldn't refuse to see you."

He knew that it would be useless to go to Damont. If he knew, he'd never tell the truth. He decided that he'd have to wait and hope that sometime he'd meet Elise on the street. Perhaps he could get some explanation from her then. He thought of everything that he could as a reason for her strange behavior, but nothing could give him any light upon the subject.

CHAPTER 22

Chief Eagle Feather was on his way to New Orleans. Accompanying him was his daughter, White Dove, the Indian wife of Damont.

For some time there had been unrest and a smoldering desire for action against the whites among the Indians who had been friendly for so long. The Tchouchoumas, vestige of the once great river tribe of the Houmas, the Chickasaws and the Chouachas, all made their living by trapping. Recently their trapping grounds had been invaded by some of the new settlers in the colony and this encroachment added fuel to their seething unrest.

For a long time these tribes, as well as the Natchez and the Punicas, had suffered from French tyranny. The massacre at Fort Rosalie was accomplished in retaliation for that tyranny and injustice. It was their one great desire to drive the settlers back beyond the river to the coast or to wipe them out altogether. The dread coalition of the tribes was nearer accomplishment than it had ever been before, and Chief Eagle Feather knew that it would take but a spark to start the flame of murder and torture and pillage which would cause untold suffering, if not annihilation of the colonists. He had just become chief of his tribe, the Chouachas, who lived above the city on the Bayou St. Jean. He had been one of the most prosperous trappers in the settlement and he was concerned over the situation, not only because of the danger to the whites with whom he had always been friendly, but because it was robbing him of some of his most profitable trapping territory. He was determined to go to Bienville and warn him of the consequences if this situation was not remedied.

When he set out upon his trip to the city, White Dove informed her father that she was going with him. She had married Damont when her father was away on one of his trapping expeditions and though he was angry at first, he accepted the situation when he realized how much his daughter loved the white man. In the beginning of their marriage Damont visited the village frequently, though he always came at night. He explained glibly to White Dove his reasons for not accepting her publicly as some of the settlers had done. He told her that when he had obtained the position in the government that he hoped to occupy, that he would take her to the city and give her the kind of life she would be entitled to as his wife. She was content to accept his lies and satisfied to let their relationship remain as it was. She was not anxious to leave her people and she was happy to know that she belonged to him and that she saw him at frequent intervals. One of his stipulations had been that she should not come to the city. He told her that other men would see her and want her, that there would be trouble and that this might harm them both, but more important, it might endanger his political ambitions. She knew nothing of politics and she accepted his reason for not wanting her to be seen by others, for his suave flattery pleased her and made her happy.

Eagle Feather accepted the situation without question. The ways of white men with their women were strange and he did not try to understand them. As long as his daughter was happy, he was satisfied, for he had more important things to think of.

When Elise had appeared upon the scene and Damont's visits suddenly ceased, White Dove had become more and more anxious and unhappy. Still willing to obey Damont's demand that she stay out of the city, she did not try to see him. The Indian maid Takona, who had worked for Madame Romain had given her the first information about Elise. Her heart was torn between bitterness and disappointment toward Damont and jealous hatred of the white girl who was trying to rob her of the man she loved, but she could do nothing until after her baby was born. It was then that she had gone to the city in search of Damont and had met him with Elise. After this meeting she hoped in vain that Damont would come to her. In the meantime the fever came, and then her baby became ill with a lingering illness and finally died. It was just after the death of her baby that Eagle Feather became chief of the tribe and the trouble arose about the trapping grounds. When he announced that he was going to the city, she said she'd go with him.

"Why do you want to go?" he asked. "What I'm going there for is no woman's business."

"I shall not bother you," she informed him. "I am going to see my husband."

"Why do you want to bother with him? He hasn't been near you in many moons. He never came near when his child was born and he left you to grieve alone when the child died. Why do you want to see him? You'd best forget him."

"Perhaps I shall," she said morosely, "after I've seen him and talked with him."

"Talking to him will do no good. If he is tired of

you what can you do to make him want you again? I told you it would be this way when you married him. It's what has happened to so many others before. But what can we do about it?" he added bitterly. "We must accept the white man's attentions to our women and not murmur when they tire of them and leave them broken-hearted. It's what I didn't want to see happen to you, my daughter," he added with a faint note of gentleness in his heavy, grave voice.

"I'm not willing to believe that it has happened to me yet, my father," she replied. "That is why I want to see him. I shall go to the city today. Will you let me go with you?"

He stared at her for a moment in silence. This was not the way for an Indian girl to answer her father. This was what her marriage had done for her, he reflected.

"You may go with me," he finally said.

It was late afternoon when they reached the city. Eagle Feather had left her at the Rampart, continuing his way down toward the governor's office.

White Dove had not told him the truth about her reason for coming to the city. She had a mission to perform before she tried to find her husband. She wasn't sure that she wanted to see Damont at all just now. Something else would have to be settled before she talked to him. First she would settle her account with this white girl who had taken her husband from her, who had kept him from coming to see his little child and had kept him away when her heart was so torn with grief. This white girl must die. Perhaps then her husband would come back to her and restore the joy she had once experienced in his love.

Takona had told her where Elise lived. She remembered the little tumbled down cottage on the edge of town. It was where the trail ended and the narrow streets of the city began behind the Rampart.

There was a thick clump of woods between the cottage and the beginning of Dumaine street, cutting the cottage off from the more thickly populated section of the street. She had been there before Elise had come to the city, when Takona worked for Madame.

She went to the door of the cottage and knocked. Madame answered her knock. White Dove asked to see the white girl who lived there. Madame told her that Elise was not there and that she would perhaps be away for an hour or so longer.

"Would you like to wait for her?" Madame asked hospitably.

"No. I will come back," White Dove said.

She left the house and wandered down the street toward the thicket. Perhaps the girl would come along this way again. It was farther down this street that she had met them before. If she should meet the girl alone here, that would be better than meeting her at the house. If she should have to go back to the house, she would bring her here. This would be a better place for what she had in mind than out in the open. No one need ever know then if she succeeded in her plan. But she didn't care whether anyone knew or not. If Damont was lost to her, it wouldn't matter what became of her. There was nothing left for which to live. She felt that he would never come back to her. When once a white man tired of his squaw, he never came back.

She was so lost in her bitter reverie that she forgot the passing of time. She didn't know how long she waited there and she didn't notice the approach of Damont until he was almost upon her.

"What are you doing here?" he asked in alarm. "I thought I told you not to come here."

"You told me many things I wish to forget," she said after the first startled moment. There was no time for her to escape or she would have hidden herself from him. She was angry and upset over this unexpected complication.

"I told you I would come to you as soon as I could. Things have come up that have kept me from doing that. But I will come, I promise. Now go home and be a good girl."

He was desperately afraid that Elise might come this way and see them together. His guilty conscience told him that she would remember the former meeting and question his behavior. He must get her away from here before that happened.

White Dove gazed at him with her grave dark eyes and said, in her halting French, "I don't go until I have talk with white girl. I told you to keep away from her. You belong to me. I told you about your little Singing Water. You not care enough to come to see her. She dead now, and you never see. Now I don't care if you never come. But I tell white girl what you are. I make her hate you as you make me hate you. If you love her, I make you suffer as you make me suffer."

"You're not going to tell her anything," cried Damont desperately. "Go on back home before I make you sorry you came here."

"I don't go," she said stoically, with a lift of her chin.

He advanced toward her as if to strike her, but she backed away from him and pulled out the keen-edged knife she had hidden in her belt.

"If you touch me, I kill you," she stated flatly.

"What are you doing with that knife?" he cried, surprised at its sudden appearance.

She didn't answer but stared at him with eyes which suddenly blazed with a light he had never seen there before. There was cold ruthless purpose in her eyes and in the expression upon her face.

"You were going to kill her with it. Is that what

you planned to do?" The horrifying truth dawned upon him with sudden force. That was why she was waiting here. She knew that Elise would pass this way.

He made a sudden lunge for the knife, but she was too quick for him and the knife evaded his grasp. He caught hold of her arm and began to twist it slowly until she was forced by the sheer pain of it to let go her hold upon the knife. He stooped and picked up the knife and plunged it into her body as she turned to ward off the blow. With a moan and a gurgling gasp, she sank to the ground and lay still. After one horrified look at her, Damont fled down the street, turned a corner and was lost to sight. He felt sure that no one had seen him, for that section of the town was deserted. He felt reasonably safe from any suspicion of murder. After he had turned the corner, he walked along leisurely until he came to his home. Once inside, he sank upon a chair and succumbed to the reaction of the shock from what had happened. There was no remorse for what he had done, only fear that in some way he might be connected with the crime. He experienced a measure of relief over the death of the girl who had proved a menace to his plans. His one hope was that he could marry Elise before some other hindrance appeared.

Elise had been delivering some sewing when White Dove had called at the cottage. She was hurrying home, for she had a dress to finish that evening. As she came along the street, she barely missed seeing Damont turning a far corner. When she left the end of the street and entered the path that led through the little thicket, she heard a faint groan and then saw the body of the Indian girl lying beside the path. She hastened to her and knelt beside her, then she saw the knife plunged into her side. She uttered a startled cry and knelt there in shocked amazement for a moment. As White Dove groaned faintly again, she put forth a trembling hand and began to draw the knife from the girl's side. There was a sharp cry of pain from the girl and a spurt of blood covered Elise's hand which held the knife.

White Dove opened her eyes, the glaze of death upon them, and stared unseeing at Elise. Then, slowly recognition came to her. She made a feeble effort to rise.

"You! You!" she cried with a sudden burst of strength. "You did — this. You — made — him — love — you." The voice was suddenly still, and her head fell back limply upon the blood-soaked ground.

Elise began to sob as she stared at the girl's lifeless body. She didn't realize that she still held the knife in her blood-stained hand, nor that she was sobbing aloud. She didn't see the dark form which glided so silently from the thicket and fled down the street with the faint patter of moccasined feet. Her mind was intent upon but one thought. This must be Andre's wife. The girl's words told her that. Somehow she must have known the truth about Andre and herself. A terrible suspicion began to fill Elise with its horror: *Andre must have killed her!* Who else could have done this awful thing? Agony filled her soul, and sobs shook her body as the suspicion became a reality in her mind.

Down the street toward the governor's office Takona sped. She had used the venom of her hatred toward Elise by rousing White Dove's jealousy against her and had stirred within her the desire for revenge. When White Dove and her father had left for New Orleans, she had followed them, hoping that she could witness whatever might transpire. She had not dared follow too closely and had arrived at the cottage after White Dove had left. As she continued on her way to town, she had caught sight of White Dove waiting in the thicket for Elise. She hid herself and waited. She saw and heard what passed between Damont and White Dove, but the sudden end of the meeting came as such a shock that it left her dazed with horror while Damont made his escape. When she recovered enough to come from her hiding place into the path, she saw Elise in the distance. She slipped back into the undergrowth again and awaited developments.

While Elise bent over the dying girl a cunning scheme came to Takona. She slipped out and fled in search of Eagle Feather. She had gone about half way toward the river when she met Eagle Feather returning from his interview with Bienville. He had finished his business much sooner than he had expected and to his entire satisfaction. He had Bienville's assurance that the trappers would be prohibited from encroaching upon the Indian trapping grounds.

Takona informed him breathlessly that his daughter had been murdered.

"The white girl has killed her with her own knife," she told him. "Hurry and you will find her there weeping over the one she killed."

Elise did not hear their approach. She was lost in an agony of her own suspicions. She did not know they were there until a pair of hands seized her and jerked her to her feet.

"You kill my White Dove!" the harsh voice of the Indian screamed. "You die for it!"

"No! No!" she wailed. "I didn't kill her. I found her there. I tried to help her!" Sobs choked her and the tears rained down her face.

"You kill her! I saw you." Elise turned her tear-filled eyes and gazed into the face of Takona. There was a glitter in her eyes and a leer of triumph upon her dark face.

"You know that isn't true," Elise cried brokenly.

"Enough talk," Eagle Feather said abruptly. "We go to Bienville. You die for this. Come."

He took one look at the dead girl lying there and only the tightening of the muscles of his jaw betrayed the sorrow which possessed him. Grasping Elise's arm with a grip of steel and motioning to Takona to come with him, Eagle Feather turned toward Bienville's office. Elise still held the blood-stained knife. None of them realized that she still held it.

CHAPTER 23

Bienville stared in amazement at the trio entering the room: Eagle Feather, dark face grim and vengeful as he gripped Elise's arm; Elise white and shaken, with something deeper than terror in her eyes; Takona, dark eyes fastened upon the white girl with a look of triumph.

"What's the meaning of this?" Bienville demanded as the group strode toward him.

"This girl kill my daughter," the Indian stated, trying to suppress his fury. "With that knife," he added, pointing to the knife Elise still held in her hand.

Bienville glanced at it, and Elise's dazed eyes followed his; then she let go. The knife fell to the floor with a thud.

"What have you to say, Mademoiselle?" Bienville asked, recognizing her and unable to believe the Indian's story. He had heard of her many acts of mercy during the epidemic. These stories didn't fit in with this gruesome one the Indian told.

She stared at him with eyes that smote him with the suffering he saw in their dark depths. She was thinking of Andre and what this murder would mean to him if the truth should become known. She shook her head slowly and said, "I didn't kill her. I could never kill anyone."

"This girl saw her," Eagle Feather rasped in guttural tones.

"Tell me what you saw," Bienville said, turning to Takona.

"I see them arguing. They fight for knife. This girl get it, strike White Dove in side. Just before she die I hear her say, 'You did this.' Then I run to get her father. When we come there this girl still kneeling beside body and knife still in her hand."

"Is this true?" Bienville asked Elise.

"No, it isn't," but her voice was so low and there was such hopeless sorrow in it that her denial wasn't convincing. "I found her lying beside the path with the knife in her side. I knelt by her and tried to remove the knife. Then she saw me and said those words. But I didn't do it."

"What do you say?" demanded Eagle Feather of Bienville.

"She will have to be tried for murder," Bienville sighed heavily.

"No! Kill her now," cried the Indian in angry voice. "I kill her back there on the path, but I want her to hang in public square where many of my people hanged. You say you want justice for my people. Let me see it done. Kill this girl who kill my daughter. Then I believe you."

"She can't be executed until she has had a fair trial," said Bienville firmly. "We shall see that justice is administered both to her and to you."

"When?" asked Eagle Feather.

"As soon as we can, according to our laws. In the meantime, Mademoiselle," he said regretfully, "we shall have to place you under arrest."

Bienville turned to Eagle Feather. "I shall send one of my officers back with you to view the body and make his report, then you may take it with you. We shall let you know when the trial takes place. But we shall keep the girl here as a witness. We can't turn her loose and run the risk of her disappearing before the trial."

Takona uttered a startled protest, but Eagle Feather silenced her. "You stay here. See that white girl kept in prison till I return." He turned to Bienville and said threateningly, "She kill my daughter. If she go free, there will be trouble. My people not forget this." Turning, he strode from the room.

Bienville eyed the two girls standing before him, Elise with white face and downcast eyes, Takona with a glitter of hate in hers as she looked at the governor and then at the white girl.

"I'm sorry, Mademoiselle, but I shall have to lock you up," he said.

"Yes, I understand," she said in low tones.

Ringing a bell, Bienville gave an order to an aide who entered and the two girls were led away to the one small jail in town. Alone at last, Elise sat down upon the small stool in her cell and tried to think calmly, but her thoughts refused to obey her effort. She could think of but one thing and that thought brought renewed suffering and added confusion. No one else could have murdered the girl but Andre. And she had had such high hopes of one day winning him for her Lord! She had built her hope of happiness upon being able one day to become his wife. She had thought him so fine and lovable in spite of the reckless life he had lived, in spite of his utter ignorance of spiritual truths. And now she knew him for what he was. A cheat who would have married her while married to another, a heartless murderer who killed in order to remove the innocent hindrance to his desires. He must have been afraid that White Dove would tell her the truth.

In the turmoil her mind was in, she never once connected the other Andre with the Indian girl, even though she remembered her former meeting with the girl. She could think of nothing else but that Andre Chenier was the guilty one. If he were discovered and tried for this murder, he would be hanged and would go out into eternity a lost soul. The thought brought a paroxysm of tears which relieved the tension somewhat. At last she lay upon the soiled cot and closed her eyes, utterly exhausted. She slept only periodically.

Bienville sent for Damont and told him what had happened. Damont listened while he struggled to keep from betraying the emotions which overwhelmed him. Consternation and fear and fury at the utter frustration of all his plans surged through him in a whirling storm of emotions. His lips were dry and parched and his hands trembled, while his eyes dared not meet Bienville's lest they betray him.

"Surely you don't believe she did such a thing as that," he finally managed to say, though his voice sounded none too steady to his own ears.

"It is hard to believe, but there's the Indian girl's testimony. She claims she witnessed the whole affair. The only thing that bothers me is that she seemed to be just a little too eager to give her testimony. There was an air of triumph about her which puzzles me."

"You say she claims to have witnessed the whole affair? Where did she say she was?" asked Damont as new fears took possession of him. *What if she saw the whole thing? His life was in her hands, if she should decide to tell the truth. Why is she telling this lie?*

"I don't know. I didn't ask her. That will all come out at the trial."

"When will that be?"

"As soon as it can be arranged. We've got to get this thing over with before that Indian stirs up trouble as he threatened. This is a pretty difficult situation for us to be in just now."

"And if she is found guilty?" asked Damont in tones which he strove to keep steady.

"She will be hanged according to the law."

"No! You couldn't do that!" he cried aghast. "Such a thing has never been done before. You couldn't kill her."

"I should hate to, but if it meant her life or the lives of thousands, I should be forced to carry out the law. That Indian was so furious that I know he'd stir up trouble if we failed to carry out the law."

After Damont left Bienville's office, he walked for a long time trying to still the battle that raged within him. It was his life or hers, he told himself, as he fought against the terror that possessed him. It was one thing to be killed in the heat of conflict or by accident, but to dangle at the end of a rope, to sit waiting to face a death like that was quite another. It took more courage than he possessed. She was lost to him now, he told himself desperately. He'd rather see her dead than to belong to someone else. Even though she died for his crime, it would be better than giving himself up and facing that death himself. The utter baseness of his nature gained control of him. He finally retraced his steps and returned to Bienville. Asking for permission to see Elise, he was told that he could see her the next day.

His heart smote him when he saw her sitting there so quietly, such a picture of utter dejection and helplessness, but he steeled his heart to the faint voice of conscience which stirred within.

"Elise, my dear," he said in tones of concern, "I came as soon as I could after hearing the terrible news. Oh, my dearest, isn't there anything that I can do to help you? I'd give my life to get you out of this terrible situation."

She smiled faintly as she said, "It was good of you to come, Monsieur. There is nothing you can do to help me, but I wish you would do something to help Madame. She must be frantic to know what has happened to me. Could you go to Annette? Perhaps she will do something for her. I have a little money. Enough to keep her for a little while."

Her lip trembled and she fought back the tears which welled up in her eyes.

"Of course. I shall be glad to see that she is taken care of. Don't worry about her anymore. And I shall do everything in my power to get you out of this."

"You're so kind," she murmured. "I'm so grateful."

He left soon afterwards, for he couldn't stand there much longer and look into her trusting eyes.

Chenier got a permit to see Elise as soon as he heard of the arrest. When he came to the door of her cell and the guard announced him she said, "I don't want to see him. Take him away."

"Elise!" cried Chenier in agony. "Let me talk to you. Tell me what has happened to turn you against me. Tell me. Please!"

She clenched her hands into tight little knots to keep from crying out to him all the agony of her love and disappointment but she said in low, firm tones, "Go away. I don't want to talk to you. Don't try to come here again. I don't want to see you."

The guard motioned to Chenier to leave. After one moment of hesitation, he followed him outside. Chenier next sought Damont again and demanded to know what had happened to turn Elise against him so suddenly and so bitterly. He knew that some lie had been told her by someone and he had a suspicion that it had been Damont, but he could get no satisfaction from him.

"I haven't the least idea," Damont told him. "I assure you I had nothing to do with it. I know you won't believe me, but it's the truth. We had better be trying to get her out of this thing instead of quarreling over something neither of us know anything about."

Chenier was forced to admit the truth of that and left, trying desperately to still the feeling of despair which swept through him. There was nothing he could do. He realized the seriousness of her plight and all that this thing involved between the Indians and the colonists; and he knew that the Indian girl's testimony, no matter how false, would stand the test of a trial. For the first time since he had become saved, he went to his knees and sought the only One who could possibly help.

"God in heaven, have mercy," he groaned. "You know she couldn't kill anyone, so don't let them hang her. You can do anything, so help her, for no one else can. I love her so much, God, and I'll spend the rest of my life trying to make her happy and trying to show You my gratitude."

He felt more at peace when he had finished this simple prayer, but during the next days, when the time for the trial arrived and no help came, he felt despair again overwhelming him.

Elise was sorry she had not asked Damont to get her Bible for her. She was hoping that he would come again so that she could ask him to get it, but he didn't have the courage to face her again. The sorrow in her eyes haunted him day and night, and though he didn't suspect the cause of the sorrow, it filled him with a feverish unrest from which he could get no relief. He couldn't eat and he couldn't sleep; his face became more thin and colorless than ever and in his pale eyes there gleamed a harrowed light which his associates attributed to his worry over the girl so soon to be tried for her life. He was the living embodiment of the truth of God's word that the wicked are like the troubled sea that cannot rest, whose waters cast up dirt and mire.

Elise realized that the evidence against her, even though false, would be enough to send her to the gallows. She had never heard of a woman being executed in the colony before, but she knew the situation and realized her danger fully. The thought of death by hanging brought a tremor of fear, for the agony, even though brief, must precede that death.

Even in the face of this agony she found peace in the knowledge that the Lord would give her strength to bear it. There came to her as a glimmer of light through the starless darkness, the memory of that verse which she had taken as her promise on the night which seemed so long ago: "In the way of righteousness there is life and in the pathway thereof there is no death."

Her life had indeed gone through strange paths, but God had protected her. Was it to end now like this? But the promise said here was no death. Perhaps it was but the entrance to eternal life. It didn't matter now, for all the joy of life was gone. What was there to live for? Just Madame, and Madame probably wouldn't be long in following her. She was glad that she had been permitted to lead a few people to the knowledge of Christ. If only she could have led Andre before he had done this terrible thing! Perhaps if she died in his place he would realize what it meant to have someone die for his sin.

How can he let me die for him, she wondered. *How can he be such a coward?* She could only pray that in some way God might touch his heart and make him see what Christ did when He died for his sins. If it would mean his salvation, then she would be glad to go, for then one day they should meet again.

CHAPTER 24

The trial brought a wave of excitement which rolled through the whole city. The court room was crowded to capacity and those who couldn't get in stood outside, milling about, trying to get a look through windows or doors. Eagle Feather came with members of his tribe and others from neighboring tribes. They were easily distinguished by their different markings and head dresses.

Bienville knew that Eagle Feather had brought these others to prove to him that there would be trouble if the trial did not go according to his judgment. He realized the seriousness of the situation. If this girl was not executed, there would be bloodshed such as there never had been since the colony was first founded. It would be worse than the massacre of Fort Rosalie, for this time the dreaded coalition of the tribes would be an accomplished fact. He knew enough of Indian markings to note that some of those who accompanied Eagle Feather were from the Punicas, Choctaws, Natchez, Chickasaws. There were others whose markings were unfamiliar to him, but he knew that they had come from farther west. Eagle Feather had done his work well in bulwarking his threat. One girl's life against the life of the colony —

that was the issue. As the governor looked at Elise his heart smote him with regret. Even though he felt that the evidence arrayed against her had a false ring to it, he knew that he would never be able to pierce through that falseness. There could be but one end to the trial. If this girl were convicted, she would have to hang.

Elise had come quietly into the room and had taken her place in the prisoner's docket. Her face was pale but there was a calmness and a poise about her that brought tears to many of the eyes fastened upon her. Some of these people she had nursed through their attack of fever. Some of them she had tried to comfort when they were in despair over the loss of loved ones. Annette was there and she was crying, unashamed. She had tried to see Elise but could not. Now she had gotten as close to her as she could. Elise caught her eye for a moment and smiled at her; and the smile brought a fresh burst of tears from Annette. Annette had spent much time in prayer since she had heard of the arrest, but as she sat there now and listened to the opening of the court proceedings, she felt as if all hope had left and that for some reason God wasn't going to answer her prayers.

Elise's eyes searched the crowd for a glimpse of Chenier. She wondered if he would have the courage to watch while she was tried for his crime. She wondered if he would be coward enough to let her go through with this and give her life for what he had done. If this would only be the means of saving him! If he could only see in this what it meant for the Son of God to die for his sin. If there was some way by which she could tell him this, it would be so much easier to die. Then she saw him sitting in a far corner; and the look in his eyes brought a stab of pain to her heart, for she realized in that brief moment that, despicable though he might be, she loved him.

She listened apathetically as the trial proceeded, for this sudden insight into her own heart disturbed her more than what Takona was saying. Takona was repeating what she had told Bienville. Questioning and cross-questioning failed to shake her story. She had heard the two quarreling, and then they fought for the knife which White Dove had in her belt. She was asked why White Dove carried the knife, and she could only reply that she didn't know. The lawyer which Bienville had appointed for the defense tried to prove that Elise killed in self-defense. Takona maintained that there had been no threat made by White Dove.

The question was then brought up as to what had caused the quarrel. At this point, Eagle Feather, in defiance of court proceedings and a word of protest from the judge, stalked forward and spoke.

"This girl here took my daughter's husband from her. She made him forget that he had a wife and a child. He forgot my girl and his child for this woman. When my White Dove's little papoose died, he never came near her because this woman had taken him from her. My White Dove came here that day to see her husband, and beg him to come back to her. This girl came upon her, and killed her. Now you kill her or we fight. You say you give justice to Indians. We want to see it now. We see it or we fight." He spoke in amazingly good French.

"Who was this man your daughter claimed as her husband?" asked Elise's lawyer, also ignoring court proceedings.

"She call him Andre," Eagle Feather announced.

"Don't you know his last name?" asked the lawyer in surprise.

"No."

"It's unbelievable that you shouldn't know the name

of the man your daughter married," the lawyer retorted.

"What does a white man's name matter?" said Eagle Feather scornfully. "She married him while I was away. She was happy, so what did it matter? I knew that sooner or later he'd forget her. They always do." His contemptuous glance swept over the audience.

"His name was Chenier," Takona informed the court.

"That's a lie!" cried Chenier jumping to his feet and striding to the front. "I never married any Indian, and I don't know this murdered girl. If the fellow who married her said his name was Chenier, then someone else used my name."

"Do you recognize this man as the one who married your daughter?" asked the lawyer. The usual proceedings of this primitive court were forgotten by everyone in the face of this unusual and dangerous situation.

"No," replied Eagle Feather. "I wouldn't know the man if I saw him. He always came to village at night. He wore *coureur de bois* outfit. Cap hid his face. I suppose he saw to that."

The lawyer turned to Takona. "Do you know this man? Is he the one who was married to the slain girl?"

Takona shrugged her shoulders. "I never saw him. He come and go like thief. White Dove say there were reasons why he not want to be known. She satisfied to have it that way. Why should I bother?"

Chenier turned and saw Damont in the back of the room. A sudden suspicion came to him. "Get that man back there," he almost shouted. "See if these Indians know him."

"Monsieur!" cried Bienville. "That is Monsieur Damont."

"I know it is. What of it? His name is Andre as well as mine. I have a suspicion that he was using my name to cover up his marriage to this girl."

"Monsieur Damont, I regret this," apologized the judge, "but we must get to the bottom of this, if possible. Would you mind coming forward?"

Outwardly Damont was calm and dignified, but inwardly every nerve was taut and tingling with fear and torment. Without venturing to look at Elise, he took his place in front of the judge.

The judge turned to Eagle Feather. "Can you identify this man?" he asked.

Eagle Feather shook his head.

The judge addressed Takona. "Can you identify this man?"

Damont turned a shade paler. If she had witnessed that scene, as she claimed, then she knew the truth. His life hung in the balance, upon her answer.

She looked him over. He could see the leer in her half-closed eyes, and he fancied he could detect a faint smile upon her lips as she shook her head and said, "No."

"What difference does it make which man marry my daughter?" Eagle Feather cried, interrupting again. "She is dead. This girl killed her. She is the one who must hang, not one of these."

The judge motioned to the two men, and they went back to their places as the proceedings were resumed. Chenier had tried to catch Elise's eye, but she had refused to look at him. She sat with her eyes fastened upon Eagle Feather's face. Only her hands tightly gripping the chair betrayed the strain she was enduring. Damont did not look her way but went back to his place and dropped into his chair. He was weak and shaken, though he maintained his outward calm.

Elise scarcely heard the rest of the proceedings. She was so exhausted and so bewildered that she couldn't think clearly, her thoughts kept revolving around the scene that she had just witnessed. There was something strange about this affair, something which she was trying to make clear in her own mind. One of these two had murdered White Dove. Was it Andre she loved or was it the other Andre? She remembered with a pang, Rosalie's words. It couldn't be Damont. Yet — and there was a sudden flash of hope within her. Rosalie hadn't said it was Chenier. She had said it was Andre. Perhaps, after all, it was Damont. The judge's words interrupted her wildly racing thoughts.

"Mademoiselle, it is with regret that the court finds you guilty of the murder of this girl. You will stand while I pronounce sentence."

After a moment's hesitation she stood and faced the court. Her eyes met those of the judge with such a clear look of calm that he lowered his gaze, unable to meet that look.

He cleared his throat and began in a sing-song voice, as if he were repeating words which were reluctant to come, "It is the duty of this court to pronounce the prisoner guilty of murder in the first degree. According to the laws of this colony, you shall be hanged by the neck until you are dead."

"When will this be?" cried Eagle Feather again disregarding court order.

"You will be quiet until this court is dismissed," the judge told him angrily. "The demands of justice will be administered in due order."

"She shall hang today! You seek to fool us with your promises of justice. Let her hang today!"

"That cannot be done," the judge insisted. "A day must be set and the decree of the court carried out according to the law. We never execute prisoners the same day they are sentenced."

"Either hang her today or we fight. We have been

fooled by you French too many times. Those men back there are from six of largest tribes in our territory. Keep your word. Hang her while we can see or we kill many white people. We drive them from our land."

Bienville leaned over to consult with the judge and the members of his staff who were present. It angered him to know that he was being put in such a position before his people. He was thinking of the girl standing there so calm and quiet in the midst of this wrangle. Somehow he couldn't believe her guilty of this crime, but he could not disregard the evidence of the court. Her simple testimony at the beginning of the trial had convinced him that she was telling the truth, but he knew there was nothing he could do to save her.

While he was conferring with the others in low tones, Elise suddenly broke the silence. "Your honor," she said in a voice which seemed to have no fear in it, "I beg of you to obey the demands of this Indian. If I am to die for a crime which I didn't commit, what does it matter whether I die today or tomorrow? The sooner I go, the better for everyone, most of all for the one who committed this murder."

As Bienville stared at her in wonder, she turned and her gaze swept slowly over the room. She was looking for Chenier. Her eyes rested upon him for a brief moment and in them was such contempt and such sorrow that he rose to his feet, impulsively bent upon going to her and begging her to believe that he couldn't have done this dastardly thing. Before he could do this, however, something happened which stopped him.

Elise had let her gaze wander to where Damont sat across the room from Chenier. What she saw in his haggard face and his blood shot eyes told her much. The light of revelation suddenly shown from her eyes as they met his harrowed gaze and her lips parted while she drew in her breath sharply.

Damont stared at her, fascinated; then he saw that she knew. A tremor shook him as he sat there hesitating. Suddenly he got to his feet and walked heavily toward the judge's stand.

"If it please the court," he began, "I have something to say."

The judge waved him aside, but he turned to Bienville and said, "Your Excellency, I am the guilty one. I killed the Indian girl. Mademoiselle Demarest is innocent."

"What?" cried Bienville. The word was a startled cry that rang through the room, and brought the echo of a gasp from the packed audience.

"I married White Dove before Mademoiselle came to the colony. I fell in love with Mademoiselle the first time I saw her, but I knew that if she ever found out that I had married another, she would never marry me. I met White Dove on the path that day, and she told me that she was going to tell Mademoiselle the truth. She threatened me with the knife when I tried to stop her from going to Mademoiselle. I got it from her and killed her. I never dreamed that it would end this way. I thought I would never be suspected. I never dreamed that she would have to pay for my crime."

"And you sat there all through this trial and let her suffer for what you had done!" There was such disdain in Bienville's voice that a flush of shame mounted to Damont's pale face.

He bowed his head and said weakly, "I was hoping until just now that there would be some way out."

"You used another man's name when you married this girl. Is that true?" asked Bienville, his anger growing.

Damont nodded. "I'm willing to pay for my crime," he said.

Eagle Feather strode to him. "So you killed my White Dove!" he cried in harsh tones of fury. "You killed her after you made her love you! After you left her to grieve alone! And you hid behind a woman! You would let her die in your place!"

Damont met the cold gaze of fury silently. Suddenly Eagle Feather's hand went to his side. With one swift movement he raised his hand, and the long keen blade of a knife flashed for a moment in the sunlight filtering through the windows; then it plunged into Damont's breast. It all happened so quickly that it was over before anyone realized what was taking place. Damont sank to the floor, blood staining the white front of his shirt, Eagle Feather marched from the room followed by his Indian cohorts. No one tried to stop him as they went out and marched out of sight. No one dared to stop them.

Elise uttered a faint cry as she saw Damont fall. She rushed to him and knelt by his side. He looked at her through eyes that were dimming as a trickle of blood oozed through his pale lips.

"Can — you — forgive?" he said slowly as he gasped weakly for breath.

"Oh, Monseiur, don't think of my forgiveness," she cried. "Ask God to forgive you before it's too late. He's your judge, not I. Don't go out into eternity without His forgiveness."

He shook his head weakly. "Too late," he gasped. "You tried but I — wouldn't — listen. I loved — you — so!" a light flashed for a moment in his dim eyes.

"But God loves you and He'll save you even yet, if you'll just ask Him," she cried, tears streaming down her face. She clasped her hands in an agony of entreaty. "Oh, call upon Him before it's too late! Please! Please!"

"It's — already — too — late." With a sudden gasp and one last look into her tear-filled eyes, he gave a slight shudder and lay still.

Only her sobs broke the silence in the room.

Chenier came to her, put his arm around her, lifting her to her feet. "Come, my dear, let's get out of here. There's nothing more you can do," he whispered, and led her unresisting from the room.

Out upon the street they were silent as they walked slowly toward the cottage. Chenier withdrew his arm from her, but she clung to him weakly as they walked. She was utterly spent from the shock and the strain of the ordeal.

"Let's not talk until we get home," she said when he started to say something. "Home! How sweet that name sounds. I never thought I'd love it as I do. Give me time to think, for there is much that we have to say after I've had a little moment to rest."

When they reached the spot where she had found White Dove, she stopped for a moment and a shudder shook her as she stood there.

"I shall never pass here without remembering," she said solemnly. "Two souls gone into eternity lost. And I the cause."

He drew her gently away from the place. "You were not to blame. You couldn't help what happened. Let's get to the house and sit down. There is much I want to tell you."

When they reached the cottage, Madame came out to meet them. She had seen them coming. She was watching for Annette. Annette had persuaded her not to attend the trial, and had promised to let her know at once what the outcome was. Madame had spent many hours upon her knees, begging for Elise's return. Now she took her in her arms and crooned over her as if she had been a little child.

"I knew the Lord would bring you back to me,"

she sobbed. "I knew He wouldn't take you away from me."

Elise hugged her and kissed the withered cheek; then she sank into the one rickety rocker. "I can't stand up any longer," she said as she laid her head back and closed her eyes.

After a while Madame left them alone.

"I want you to forgive me, Andre, for thinking such terrible things about you," Elise said humbly. "I — thought you murdered the girl and that you were letting me die for your crime."

"Yes, I know," he said heavily. "I knew it there in the court when I saw that look in your eyes. That was why you wouldn't talk to me all this time, wasn't it? You thought I was White Dove's husband."

"Yes."

"I had so much to tell you, yet you wouldn't give me a chance. If you had just heard what I had to say, then perhaps you wouldn't have thought me capable of such a crime, even though Damont had used my name when he married the girl. How did you ever find out about this marriage in the first place?"

"Tell me first what it was that you had to tell me. That's more important than anything else. We can talk about this later. What did you want to tell me?"

She saw the warm light that came into his eyes as he spoke.

"I wanted to tell you that at last I had accepted Christ as my Saviour."

"O, Andre! Andre! If I had only known! Tell me about it. It's too wonderful! Tell me!"

"I felt something the morning we left the duelling grounds. Somehow the sight of you there under the trees kneeling in prayer did something to me. I can't explain it, but your utter dependence upon God and your love for Him and trust in Him was made so real by that picture that when I got home I went to my knees and did what you had tried for so long to make me willing to do. I confessed to God that I was a lost sinner, and I asked Him to give me what you had. And He did. I wanted to tell you right away but — well, you know all that happened to keep me from seeing you. I suppose it was while you were at Damont's house that someone told you the lie about me being married to the Indian girl. Was it Damont?"

"No. It was Madame Allain."

"How did she know?" he asked in surprise.

"I don't know. But I know now that it wasn't you she was talking about, but Monsieur Damont."

He took her hand. "Elise, this may not be a good time to tell you what I've told you so often, but I can't keep from saying it. I love you so much. Could you learn to love me? I'll never be worthy of you, but I would strive to make you happy. Do you think you ever could love me?"

She smiled again. This time a warm, tender smile lighted her eyes with a glow that seemed to suffuse her face with added beauty.

"I've wanted so many times to tell you how much I loved you," she said in tones throbbing with joy, "but I dared not let you know when you still refused to accept my Lord. I've loved you for so long. It's been a struggle to keep you from knowing."

He took her in his arms; their lips met. He held her there, and she laid her head upon his shoulder with a sigh of content.

"You've no idea how I've longed to be here," she said when there was time for speech.

"And I've been aching to hold you for such a long, long time," he murmured, his cheek against hers.

Perched upon the rickety gate, a mocking bird burst into singing that was but an echo of the song of joy within their hearts.